Private Relations

THE SWINGERS 2

Private Relations

Nick Clarke

POCKET
B O O K S

New York London Toronto Sydney Tokyo Singapore

First published in Great Britain by
Pocket Books in 1993
A division of Simon & Schuster Ltd
A Paramount Communications Company

Simon & Schuster Ltd
West Garden Place
Kendal Street
London W2 2AQ

Simon & Schuster of Australia Pty Ltd
Sydney

A CIP catalogue record for this book is
available from the British Library
ISBN 0-671-71767-7

Typeset by Keyboard Services, Luton
Printed and bound in Great Britain by
HarperCollins Manufacturing, Glasgow

*This is for Johnny Gewirtz and Ronnie Dunn
– two jolly good sports.*

But pleasures are like poppies spread –
You seize the flow'r, its bloom is shed;
Or like the snow falls in the river –
A moment white, then melts for ever.

Robert Burns (1759–1796)

❀ ONE ❀

Match of the Day

White is the colour,
Football is the game,
You're a load of poofters
And Fulham is your name.

The happy Tottenham Hotspur fans sang from the terraces as their team notched their fourth goal against a distinctly lack-lustre Fulham side. Though having home advantage and the benefit of scoring first through a harsh penalty decision, they now found themselves three goals down with only ten minutes to play.

In the grandstand Martin Reece, managing director of Cable Publicity and a season ticket holder at Craven Cottage, Fulham's pleasant little stadium in West London, groaned heavily. 'I don't know why we bother coming here, I really don't,' he complained to Ivor Belling, Cable's senior account executive and fellow Fulham fan. 'Every year we spend fifty quid each on season tickets and what do we get – bloody aggravation, that's all. Look at that new centre forward, the goalie on the floor and he misses from two yards. My grannie could have scored from there and she's been dead three years.'

'No, be fair,' said Ivor thoughtfully, 'she'd have probably hit the bar. The team's getting worse, no doubt about that.' And as if to confirm his judgment, the Spurs forwards danced through a hesitant Fulham defence to score for the fifth time that afternoon.

'Come on, Ivor, I've seen enough, more than enough,'

urged Martin, rising from his seat. The two young men joined the steady trickle of Fulham fans who were making their way towards the exits. As they trudged down Stevenage Road towards Martin's car Ivor felt a sharp tap on his shoulder from a portly man in a camel hair overcoat walking briskly besides them. He turned his head to see that his assailant was none other than Cable's accountant, Harold Godfrey.

'Hello Harry, enjoy the game?' said Ivor.

'I should say so, could have been ten-one if Jimmy Greaves had really been on song,' he replied with satisfaction. 'I didn't know you two were football fans.'

Ivor gave a tiny smile. 'We're not keen on football, Harry, we're Fulham supporters,' he said wryly.

'Speak for yourself,' fumed Martin crossly. 'I've had more than enough aggravation from this lousy team. I just said to Ivor, why should I pay fifty pounds a year to get upset every Saturday?'

'You mean Cable Publicity pays fifty pounds a year', the accountant reminded him. 'I helped persuade the tax inspectors to allow your season ticket as a legitimate business expense. Believe me, that took some doing especially as this new Labour government is cracking down on business entertaining.'

'Well, you've had your reward. Spurs look like going places this season. Alf Ramsey's bound to pick Greaves and Martin Peters for the World Cup squad next year,' said Martin, fumbling in his pocket for the key of his new car. 'Anyhow, I'm giving up going to Fulham, I'd rather watch a game in the park instead.'

'You've been saying that for the last three years,' teased Ivor as they waved goodbye to Harry Godfrey. 'But you just can't change supporting a club – it's as hard as changing your newspaper or even the way you vote.'

Martin grunted as they reached his car and muttered: 'I was really looking forward to this weekend, Ivor. My wife's up in Manchester for some big conference and tonight I had planned to take out that new receptionist we took on a couple of weeks ago.'

'You're a fast worker,' said Ivor, trying to keep the disappointment out of his voice. He too had designs on the cute mini-skirted girl who wiggled her bottom whenever he passed her in the corridor.

'This is 1965, Ivor, you have to move quickly these days or you'll be left behind,' said his boss, sliding the silver Jaguar throught the crowd which was now spilling out of Craven Cottage. 'Mind, I'm a fine one to talk. Here I am off the leash on a Saturday night and I'm all dressed up and nowhere to go.'

'How about a visit to the Hunkiedorie Club? Nedis always puts on a good cabaret on Saturday nights and there'll be plenty of girls.'

'It would cost a packet – and Harry Godfrey says we can't put through any more big bills for entertaining overseas visitors as we haven't even any overseas clients on the books! I'd rather have one off the wrist than pay fifty quid for a quick fuck – and after drinking poor champagne at five quid a bottle till two in the morning. Nedis won't let the girls leave before then, you know, unless they've managed to get the punters to chalk up a bar bill for more than twenty quid.'

Ivor nodded his agreement and thought hard about his employer's predicament. It would do no harm to help his boss out, especially as he had planned to ask for five hundred a year more. However, there was no way he was going to forego his date with Samantha, a leggy blonde he had successfully chatted up at lunchtime at Yummies Sandwich Bar a few days back. 'I'm taking out a girl on a first date tonight, Martin. We're going to the National Film Theatre to see *The Blue Angel*. I could ask her if she has a friend who might make up a foursome.'

'Is this the girl you met last Wednesday? Is she pretty?'

'Yup, she's a real corker.'

3

'Is she? Then even if she has a friend, I bet she'll be a real dog. Have you noticed how pretty girls never hang around together? They always seem to pair off with less attractive birds. Perhaps it's a sort of subconscious desire to make sure they're first in the competition to attract the boys.' Martin navigated the car through Hammersmith and on to the road back to Hampstead where both men lived.

'So you don't want me to even try?' asked Ivor.

'No, I'd be grateful if you gave her a ring,' said Martin without too much enthusiasm. 'After all, we lost a client yesterday, the horses I backed this afternoon are still running at Kempton Park and Fulham have gone down five-one at home. My luck must change some time.'

'Of course it must,' agreed Ivor sympathetically. 'They say that bad things happen in threes – so who knows? Tonight could well see the bluebird of happiness shit in your lap.'

Martin grinned as he gunned the Jaguar down Ladbroke Grove towards the Northern suburbs. 'Oh dear,' said Ivor suddenly. 'I'm afraid that sodding bluebird hasn't arrived yet.'

'Why, what do you mean?'

'Slow down, there's a police car behind and he's flashing his lights at us.'

Martin clapped his hand over his forehead. He pulled over and sat resignedly as two uniformed oficers got out of their car and walked towards them. He wound down the window as they approached. One cop walked around the car checking the tax disc and registration number whilst the other came up to his door.

'Good evening, officer, is anything the matter?' he asked in as light a voice as he could muster.

'I'm afraid there is, sir – do you know what speed you were –' The policeman's jaw suddenly drooped as he looked across at Ivor. 'Blow me, it's Ivor Belling, it is you Ivor, isn't it?' Martin looked blankly as Ivor gave an

4

affirmative little smile. 'Ivor, don't you recognise me? I'm Roger Tagholm.'

Ivor peered across and clicked his fingers. 'Hello, Roger, how you doing? I didn't recognise you at first in your uniform.' He clambered out of the car and walked round to shake hands with the traffic cop. 'Roger and I met at Billy Bucknall's birthday party at the Hunkiedorie a couple of weeks ago,' he explained to Martin with a glassy grin – he had put the not inconsiderable bill on his monthly expense sheet. Strictly speaking, the evening was not spent on business, as the Club's entertainment manager had invited a few select members to celebrate his fortieth birthday with the kind of party that would have stopped the presses if any newspaper gossip columnist had been present.

'What a night that was, eh?' PC Tagholm guffawed and slapped Ivor playfully on the shoulder. 'I bet your John Thomas took a few days to recover, I know mine did!' he chortled and Ivor nodded. 'It was worth it though, wasn't it Roger?' he said. 'What did you think of Candy, that gorgeous redhead?'

The policeman smacked his lips and dug Ivor in the ribs. 'I'll tell you what though, Ivor, I found out that she was a genuine red–head! We had a quickie with her, you know, whilst that new young pop star you brought along, what was his name, Ruff Trayde, was on stage.'

'Sounds like a great party,' said Martin heavily. 'I wish Billy had invited me.' He felt doubly aggrieved. Not only had Ivor enjoyed what had obviously been a great rave-up at Cable Publicity's expense but he, his employer, had not even been told about it beforehand – even though Martin had been one of the founder members of the Hunkie-dorie, a discreet and very exclusive gentlemen's club run by a smooth Greek restauranteur, one Nedis Depocoulos. His brother-in-law, Billy Bucknall, the birthday boy, acted as master of ceremonies at the notorious Hunkiedorie cabaret shows. Nedis contributed generously to the police charities and somehow always forgot to present bills to visiting officers from his local nick – which meant that he was able to put on the raunchiest shows in London with members of the audience being encouraged to participate when called upon to do so.* The beautiful girls earned good money from the Club and even more if they wished to be taken home at the end of the evening. Nedis Depocoulos kept a happy ship. Though the Hunkiedorie Club was expensive, no customer was ever cheated. So he managed to satisfy a wealthy, influential clientele of businessmen who paid two hundred and fifty pounds a year for the privilege of membership for which there was a healthily long waiting list.

'Are you a member of the Hunkiedorie, sir?' asked PC Tagholm.

'Ever since it opened four years ago,' replied Martin and the policeman shook his head. 'But I wasn't asked to Billy's birthday thrash.'

'But you were invited, Martin,' interrupted Ivor. 'I took the call from Billy himself but it was the night you were taking your wife to the opera. So I didn't even tell you about it as I knew you'd be upset about not being able to go.'

Martin slumped in his seat. 'It never rains but it pours,' he groaned. 'My horses go down, Fulham get smashed at home, I'm stopped for speeding and now I find out I missed the chance of fucking that gorgeous new redhead.

'Still, officer, I'm glad you and Ivor enjoyed yourselves, I really am,' he added rather unconvincingly.

'Thank you sir. What a rotten day you seem to have had! What a pity, I don't like booking a Hunkiedorie member because I know how expensive it is there. I mean, I bought a round of drinks at Billy Bucknall's party and it came to over a fiver – that's much more than I'm used to paying out.'

*[See *The Swingers 1: The Mini Mob*.]

A slow grin crept over Martin's face – a speeding fine would cost him at least twenty pounds and a probable endorsement on his licence. Perhaps my luck is on the turn at last, he thought, as he tugged out his driving licence and slipped a fiver inside it.

'You'll want to check my particulars,' he said as he proferred the licence out of the window.

'H'm, yes, well that all seems to be in order, sir,' said PC Tagholm as his colleague came across with his notebook in his hand. 'No, put that book away, Jack, I've decided to let this gentleman off with a warning. Now you mind how you go, sir because next time it'll be a ticket.' And with a wink he added quietly: 'See you at the Hunkiedorie some time.' He gave Martin back his licence before walking with his partner to their car.

'What did you do, give him back the fiver he spent at the Hunkiedorie?' asked Ivor as he sat himself back in his seat. 'A bit dangerous, wasn't it?'

Martin nodded and said: 'I suppose so, but I got a result because it would cost me at least four times that in court. When we get back to your flat, ring up your girl and see if she has a friend available for tonight. At last, I'm beginning to feel just a little bit lucky!'

It was almost six o'clock by the time they reached Ivor's apartment. Strangely enough the mood of the two men had switched, with Martin Reese optimistically looking forward to the evening and Ivor Belling slightly apprehensive as he dialled Samantha's number. He let the telephone ring out and was just about to tell Ivor that the girl was not at home when Samantha's husky drawl answered him.

'Hello Sam, it's Ivor here,' he said. 'I thought you were out as the phone rang for ages. Have you just come in?'

'No, I was in the bath. Is there any problem about this evening, Ivor? I hope you're not going to let me down at the last minute.'

'Of course I'm not,' he said stoutly, and proceeded to explain how an old friend suddenly found himself free this

7

evening and wondered whether she had a girl friend who was at a loose end and who would care to make up a foursome.

There was a pause at the other end of the line and then Sam giggled. 'It's a real coincidence that you should call just now, Ivor, as I do have a friend with me at this very moment. Hold on a moment and let me ask her if she would like to double date.'

Ivor listened to the sound of muffled giggles and then Samantha came back on the line. 'Okay, Ivor, tell Martin he has a date with Katie Hatfield.'

'Fine,' said Ivor, giving Martin a thumbs-up sign. 'Will Katie be at your house, Sam? Yes? Then we'll pick you up at quarter to eight. *Ciao*.'

His boss rubbed his hands together in glee. 'I'm not superstitious but I just know that we'll score tonight, I can feel it in my water. Look, I have to go back home and change but why don't you come over to my place when you're ready and you can leave your car in my garage. As you fixed up the girls, I'll do the driving whilst Sam gives you a gobble in the back seat!'

'I should be so lucky! No rush though, Martin. Do you fancy a drink before you go?'

Martin consulted his watch. 'Yes, just time for a small Scotch please, ta. I mean, small, Ivor, because I'm driving and I'll want a glass of wine if we take the girls out for dinner afterwards.' Ivor poured a large measure for himself and a smaller one for Martin from the litre bottle of black label Johnnie Walker and handed Martin his drink. 'That copper pal of yours, Roger Tagholm, certainly enjoyed himself at Billy Bucknall's birthday party,' said Martin. 'How did you make out, Ivor? Come on, tell me all about it. Confession is good for the soul.'

Ivor grinned as he slumped down in his favourite armchair. 'Well, I musn't grumble, I suppose though I did fancy that redheaded stripper, Candy, who Roger had his wicked way with whilst Ruff Trayde was on stage. I bought Ruff and his new manager, what's his name, Tony

Mulliken, with me and we had a few drinks in the bar. We were served by a new girl who'd only been working at the Hunkiedorie for a week or so. She was a tall girl, slim and pretty with a mane of long dark hair. She was wearing a white blouse and a white mini-skirt that just about covered her bum. "Hello boys," she said. "My name is Suzie and I'll be looking after you this evening. We're pushing the boat out tonight for Billy Bucknall – all drinks are on the house till after the cabaret. So what can I get you, champagne, wine, whisky, brandy?" She pouted a bit and then she looked again at Ruff. "Oooh, I know you, you're Ruff Trayde the singer, aren't you? Can I have your autograph?" Now you know what happens if girls hear that Ruff's around so I said: "Sure, but Suzie, be a pal and don't tell the others that Ruff's here. It's a private party and he's off duty, but of course he'll sign an autograph for you, won't you, Ruff?"

"Of course," said Ruff, flashing her that smouldering look that makes them all wet their panties. Tony Mulliken handed him a publicity photograph and he scrawled his name on it. "There you go, Suzie," he said and she moved across to him with a casual swing of the hips and took the photo, thanking him with a squeeze of his arm and a kiss on the cheek. Already my cock was beginning to stir. It was clear not only that Suzie was one of those girls who just oozed sex but that she enjoyed knowing how she turned men on, especially when dressed in a provocative fine blouse which hung loose but held her boobs whilst she moved. You could see her nipples through the lace in her bra. We ordered champagne and had a great time. Thank heaven Tony Mulliken was there though, because one of the young barmen caught Ruff's eye and before you could say Jack Robinson he was chatting the guy up.'

'Christ, it's difficult enough handling a pop star's publicity,' burst out Martin. 'But only Cable Publicity has to be lumbered with a nancy-boy! If the press ever found out. . . .' His voice tailed off and he downed the rest of his Scotch. 'No problem, was there?'

'No, Tony found them in a private room and said he'd knock on the door when it was time for Ruff to come out and sing a couple of numbers. Anyhow, he bumped into the little blonde girl you had a little scene with recently.'

Martin's eyes lit up and he grinned. 'You don't mean horny Helene?'

'The very same, and once she found out he was Ruff Trayde's manager she dragged him into Nedis's office for a private demonstration of her talents. So there I was, sitting on my own when Suzie returned and gave me a dazzling smile. "Ivor Belling, I've been hearing all about you," she said, leaning against the table, her buttocks on the edge, her legs slightly apart. "It must be such fun working in publicity. Do you handle any other pop stars besides Ruff?"

'"Not at the moment," I said, looking into her deep hazel eyes, "But I can think of another account I'd love to get my hands on." She giggled and said mischievously: "Do you know something? I'll bet you've never seen the girls' changing room here, have you?"

'"No, but I hope you're going to show it to me," I said as I rose to my feet. I was trying to hide the awkward bulge in my trousers as she took my arm and guided me towards the 'Staff Only' door. Once we were safely inside she threw some coats on the floor and as we silently sank down onto the pile our lips met and we were away! I let my hands rove along her neck and shoulders but as bold as brass she took hold of my hand and moved it down to her breasts which I squeezed and fondled through the light material of her blouse. I unbuttoned her blouse and, as she shrugged it off, I unclipped her bra which followed the blouse onto the carpet.

'"What lovely breasts you have," I whispered as I squeezed the firm, fleshy globes before circling her large tawney nipples with the palms of my hands. We kissed again, our tongues twining together and I let one hand snake downwards and move up under her skirt. As I stroked the insides of her thighs she let her hand fall down

10

to my lap and she started to rub my cock which was stiffer than a starched lamppost. Now I curled one finger under the elastic of her high-cut satin panties and placed it along her long, damp crack. Suzie moaned as my finger slid lightly back and forth over her clitty and she raised her hips for me to pull down her knickers which she stepped out of as they reached her ankles. Quickly she unzipped her skirt and I tugged down my trousers and pants, releasing my prick which bounced free like a spring-loaded salami!

'"Take off all your clothes, Ivor," she murmured. "I prefer making love in the nude." So I tore off the rest of my clothes and I gazed at this gorgeous girl. Suzie was naked and she was beautiful and when she said softly: "Come on, Ivor, I want you to fuck me," it made my cock stiffen more than I thought possible.

'She lay on her back with her eyes half closed as she stroked her fingers through the silky dark hair of her thick bush. She smiled wickedly as I lowered myself on top of her and reached out to grab hold of my straining shaft. She guided it to the seething lips of her lovebox and I slid right in and began to pound away. Oh, Martin, I tell you, sliding through Suzie's juicy cunt was an amazing experience – it was like being engulfed in a quicksand of sticky, hot honey and she feverishly locked her legs around my back and I pumped in and out like a man demented. It was a short, sharp fuck but it was great for us both. I spunked great gushes of jism inside her and she came as well, shuddering into a terrific orgasm as hoarse little yelps of delight escaped her throat.

'"M'mm, that was marvellous," she said happily as I rolled off her. "But oh dear, your poor little cockie looks very sorry for itself. Do you think I can make it nice and big again?"

'"You're very welcome to try!" I gasped and she wriggled herself across me so that her bum was over my face and her dripping snatch was just over my lips. Well, of course, I began to lick her out and tasted the tangy mix of both our love juices whilst she closed her hand around my cock. It began to stiffen up and she capped and uncapped my knob, pulling down the foreskin as with the other hand she began to massage my balls. Once my tool was rock-hard again she started to nibble all around the ridges of my knob which made my whole body jerk up and down like an electric current was being passed through me. Then she opened her mouth and sucked in my shaft until it must have touched her throat. Up and down, up and down bobbed her head whilst I frantically licked and lapped at her sopping slit.

'It was the nicest *soixante neuf* I've had for some time and when she changed her sucking into a kind of erotic pattern I knew I couldn't stand it much longer. "I'm going to shoot again if you don't stop, Suzie! Do you want it in your mouth or in your cunt?"

'Athletically, she twisted herself round and parted her thighs, moaning: "Fuck me, please fuck me." I rubbed my knob against the pouting lips of her pussy and then, when I knew my cock was in the perfect position, I rammed in my shaft right in so that our pubic hairs meshed together.

'Suzie writhed away under my pistoning thrusts, swaying her hips from side to side as her fingernails clawed my back as we fucked away like crazy. Then all of a sudden I felt her body stiffen under me and I thought she was about to come but instead she moved her hands to my face and whispered: "Ivor, someone's coming."

'"Yes, me!" I croaked but she shook her head impatiently. "No! I mean outside," she said urgently. "I thought I heard the door opening behind me."

'I looked up and saw that Suzie was quite right. There, framed in the light coming in from the corridor was a man who was standing dressed only in a pair of boxer shorts through which protruded his huge hard-on. "Who's that?" I said sharply, worried that Suzie and I might both be in trouble. But fortune was with us as it was none other than Tony Mulliken, who had just fucked horny Helene and had come back into the girls' changing room to change back into the rest of his clothes. I was so relieved to see who it was that I sighed with relief and told Suzie that the intruder was only Tony, Ruff Trayde's personal manager, who had been sitting at our table. "Hi, Tony," said Suzie gaily. "Would you like to come and join the party?"

'Momentarily I had lost my concentration so that my tingling prick was moving only slightly as Tony cleared his throat and replied a little shyly: "I'd love to, so long as Ivor doesn't mind." I waved away any objection and began to jerk my hips in a slow regular rhythm as Tony pulled off his shorts and knelt down by us. Suzie edged herself up onto her elbows and looked up at him. He was holding his huge prick in his hand, pointing the pink mushroom helmet straight at her mouth. She licked her lips and said admiringly: "Wow, you didn't tell me that your friend was hung like a donkey, Ivor."

'"I didn't know myself." I growled and Tony said proudly: "Just a fraction under eleven inches" as Suzie opened her lips and jammed them over his thick shaft. So now she had the two of us taking care of her with Tony fucking her mouth as I reamed out her honeypot.

'Then I had an exciting idea. "How about us two changing places?" I asked Suzie who nodded her acceptance through her mouthful of hot, wet cock.

'Tony and I withdrew our pricks and Suzie turned herself over, resting herself on her elbows as she wriggled her dimpled little bottom lasciviously towards us. Tony then knelt behind her and stroked his straining shaft into the crevice between her bum cheeks. He leaned over and fondled her erect nips as he inserted his whopper inside her love box from behind. "Aaah, that's great," she crooned as I lay down beside her. She put out a hand and took hold of my cock, curving three fingers over the helmet with her little finger straying down along the pulsing ridge. Then she grasped my boner in both hands and began to tongue my balls as Tony began to work up a rhythm, shafting his huge truncheon in and out of her cunt from between the cheeks of her bum.

13

'This made Suzie squeal with pleasure and she pulled my cock towards her and sucked in my shaft, gobbling greedily, licking and salivating with her naughty tongue until I cried: "My God! I'm coming Suzie, I can't stop it" and I spurted a gush of sticky spunk down her throat which she gulped down with great delight.

'Tony Mulliken was also approaching boiling point and began to slew his mighty cock in and out of Suzie's squelchy cunt more quickly as the quivering girl yelled out uninhibitedly: "Now, Tony, now! Cream my cunt with your spunk, you big-cocked boy!"

'He obliged almost instantly and changed to fucking her with short, stabbing strokes as he shivered all over and then shot his load. Suzie, now totally carried away, yelled out: "I'm coming too, I'm coming, aaah, I'm coming, aaah, aaah, AAHH!"

'The three of us collapsed in a tangled heap and I noticed that Tony had spunked so much jism inside Suzie's cunt that a good deal of gooey white spunk had leaked out and had run down her thighs and onto the grey worsted coat we were lying on, soaking into the material which had also absorbed much of Suzie's love juices whilst we were enjoying ourselves.

'"Shit, look at this coat," I said, mopping my brow. "Whoever this belongs to will have some explaining to do when he gets home tonight."

'But Tony grinned and said: "What are you worried about, Ivor? It could be a lot, lot worse."

'"How on earth could it be worse?'

'"Well, for a start, it could have been one of our coats! Anyhow, serve him right, this'll teach him not to leave his coat in the girls' changing room! Still, if you feel bad about it, don't worry too much. If Suzie can find a pin somewhere I'll scribble a note and leave it on his lapel." '

As Ivor paused to swallow the rest of his drink, Martin leaned forward in his chair and said: 'What a curious thing to say! He sounds like the very nice chap who dented my car whilst parking and instead of just driving off, left a

14

card with his name and address and an apology under my windscreen wiper.'

'That's a good analogy,' agreed Ivor nodding his head sagely. 'Tony Mulliken is a very decent sort and in a way did the same thing on this occasion. After we dressed he wrote on his coat and suggested that the owner buys a bottle of Dr Jonathan Atkins' Liquid Magic, an American product which shifts almost every mark from cloth. Only a few shops stock it in this country but for certain he knew that a bottle could be bought from the all-night chemists in Wigmore Street. As he did not wish the owner of the coat to be out of pocket, Tony pinned a pound note to the letter which he fixed onto the lapel of the garment.

'"We must do this again some time," I said to Suzie and Tony as I stood by the door, tired but very happy after that wonderful love-making *à trois*.

'"Sure, all three of us. Gosh, is that the time, I must go upstairs and finish my shift," said Suzie who started to pull on her clothes. "We'd better be getting back to see that Ruff is ready for his number," said Tony and so we also hurriedly dressed and Suzie kissed us goodbye.'

'So a good time was had by all,' Martin commented with a sigh. 'I hope we'll do half as well this evening. Tell me though, didn't you join in the fun and games with Candy and PC Tagholm?'

'No, we'd both had enough for the time being and anyway Tony and I were too busy keeping an eye on Ruff, who we managed to drag away from his new friend behind the bar. Private party or not, there were one or two people at the Club that night who would have called the newspapers if they'd have found out about Ruff's little peccadillo.'

'Or even his big one,' grinned Martin evilly as he heaved himself to his feet. 'Don't forget to charge the bill to Ruff's account. After all, you were looking after him, weren't you?

'Now I'd better be off as I want to shower and shave before we meet the girls. Where are we meeting them?'

'At Sam's flat in Kilburn so I'll come round to join you after half past seven,' said Ivor as he escorted his boss to the door. 'By the way, your girl's name is Katie Hatfield. I don't know anything about her so it's a completely blind date. Don't hold me responsible if things don't work out.'

Martin waved away the warning. 'Of course I won't,' he promised whilst he slipped on his coat. 'But I'm telling you, Ivor, I'd bet a pound to a penny that this is going to be a night to remember.'

Despite his earlier optimism, Martin was distinctly uneasy by the time he parked his car outside Samantha Garrett's apartment. After all, Ivor had been bowled over by Sam and, looking coldly at the situation, the chances of her friend also being attractive were in reality very slim. However, he had nothing better to do this Saturday night and, hell's bells, it had to be worth taking the gamble. Twenty-five-to-one winners did very occasionally romp home – even though he never seemed to back them!

Still, there were butterflies in the pit of his stomach whilst he walked up the stairs to the front door. Ivor pressed the bell and even through the muzzy tone of the intercom, Sam's girlish voice sounded alluringly sexy. 'Stay where you are, Ivor, Katie and I will be down in just a minute.' Martin took a deep breath and blew out his cheeks as he heard the clatter of the girls' heels on the linoleum floor of the hall. The door swung open and his eyes brightened as Samantha Garrett came into view. God, no wonder Ivor was smitten when he saw her at Yummies, thought Martin as he smiled at the stunning girl. Sam was tall and head-turningly pretty with large, liquid blue eyes, a well shaped nose and full generous lips which parted to reveal two rows of small, sparkling white teeth. Her face was capped by a mane of golden blonde hair which she wore in a fringe over her forehead and in long, sleek strands over her ears and down over her shoulders.

'Hi, Ivor, nice to see that you're punctual. I hate to be kept waiting,' said this heavenly apparition lightly as she rummaged in her bag for her house keys. 'Now then, you must be Martin. Hello there, I'm Sam Garrett and this is my friend Katie Hatfield – Katie meet Ivor Belling and Martin, um, I'm sorry, Martin, I've forgotten your surname.'

'Reece,' said Martin as he shook her proferred hand. Sam stepped aside to allow the other girl to come out of the flat and Martin could not prevent a broad smile from creasing across his face.

Katie Hatfield was also a real cracker. Her skin colouring was as dark as Sam's was fair. Later in the evening she was to mention that her maternal grand-parents hailed from Italy. She had equally attractive looks – her high cheekbones stood out seductively in her olive skinned oval face and her soft auburn hair also tumbled down the sides of her face in the fashionably loose, long style that model Jean Shrimpton and beauty expert Mary Quant had made so popular. Katie had left her coat open and her maroon cashmere sweater accentuated the full, firm swells of her breasts whilst a short skirt of a similar colour highlighted the graceful contours of her long legs.

Martin opened the front passenger door for Katie who looked admiringly at him. 'My, my, Sam, you didn't tell me we were going out with such posh guys,' she twinkled as she made herself comfortable in the lush leather seat.

'Appearances can be deceptive,' said Ivor solemnly. 'Martin's the managing director of our company so he needs a luxurious car like a Jaguar. But you should see what senior management have to put up with, Katie. If I'm lucky, I'll swap my motor scooter for one of those new Austin Minis.'

'Ha bloody ha,' retorted Martin as Samantha and Ivor snuggled together in the back of the car. 'And if you're unlucky we'll lose an account and you'll be down to a push bike! Tell me, Katie, what do you do? Ivor told me that Sam's an articled clerk at a firm of solicitors near us in Holborn. Are you also studying law?'

'No, I'm also an articled clerk but I've hopefully only

eighteen months to go before I'm a chartered accountant.'

'An accountant?' marvelled Martin as he swung the car
into Fitzjohns Avenue, earning a blast from the horn and
a few choice words from the driver of a Ford Zodiac which
was speeding down the hill. 'And yours!' hooted back
Martin angrily. 'Some of these stupid sods think they own
the road.'

'Never mind,' soothed Katie, patting his knee with her
hand. 'In any case, what he suggested is anatomically
impossible.' Martin chuckled and replied: 'You're right,
it's daft to get all steamed up, though traffic these days
makes driving a nightmare. Still, there was no need to use
all that language – not that the air doesn't get blue at
Cable Publicity because we work under great pressure
and letting out a few ripe phrases often eases the tension.
Now that's something you professional people don't have
to deal with.'

Katie swept a lock of silky dark hair from her face. 'You
can't be serious, Martin! Why, you should hear some of
our clients when we're involved in a take-over or merger.
You could cut the atmosphere at some of those meetings.
My boss has always believed in calling a spade a spade and
often a fucking shovel when he's really riled!'

'Funny, but you don't think of accountants or lawyers
shouting the odds like we do,' ruminated Ivor, putting his
hand round Sam's shoulders. 'But probably even the
Archbishop of Canterbury says something stronger than
"oh dear" if someone catches him in the balls with
something sharp.'

'Mr Godfrey doesn't need anyone to knee him in the
balls. He effs and blinds if his coffee isn't hot enough in
the morning,' giggled Katie.

The two boys perked up their ears. 'Mr Godfrey did
you say? Not Harold Godfrey, by any chance, of Godfrey
and Smolask?' aked Ivor.

'Yes, that's right. Why, do you know him?'

'I should say so, he's been my accountant since I started

18

with Cable Publicity back in 1960!' said Martin. 'Funnily enough we saw him only this afternoon when Ivor and I bumped into him after the football.'

'What a coincidence! Well, he'll be in a good mood on Monday as Spurs won five-one. Sorry to rub it in, Sam,' laughed Katie as her friend in the back seat let out a loud groan.

'I'm a Fulham fan,' she exclaimed and turned to Ivor. 'If you and Martin start crowing about how your team thrashed us today, you can jolly well turn the car round and take us back home!'

'You follow Fulham?' exclaimed Ivor delightedly. 'But we're Fulham supporters too! Martin and I go to almost every home game.'

'Gosh, do you really?' squealed Sam. 'Oh dear, Katie, it's bad news I'm afraid – we've two guys heavily into masochism here! Later on we'll probably have to tie them to the bedposts and cane their bottoms.'

Martin guffawed as he looked at Sam's face in the mirror. 'No, I'm not that way inclined, though I'm game for whatever turns you on. I agree with the philosophy of that famous Victorian actress, what was her name now, oh yes, Mrs Patrick Campbell, said: "I don't care what consenting adults do to each other so long as they don't do it in the streets and frighten the horses!"'

'Absolutely so,' agreed Katie. This remark brought a gleam to Martin's eyes for it surely confirmed a liberal attitude which boded well for the remainder of the evening. I'll even be able to park the car near the cinema, he thought, and sure enough to his delight a van pulled out just as he was cruising along Waterloo Bridge.

'Tell me, Sam, why are we going to watch a thirty-five-year-old German movie when there are so many good brand new films to see?' asked Ivor as they walked down the steps to the National Film Theatre. 'Sam's a film buff,' said Katie gaily, slipping her arm through Martin's. 'I bet you've seen *The Blue Angel* before, haven't you?'

The blonde girl smiled sweetly and said: 'Oh yes, but I

loved the film so much I can't wait to see it again. None of you will be disappointed by it – you all know the story, don't you? It's about a fuddy-duddy professor who becomes infatuated with a low-class night club singer, played by Marlene Dietrich. You must have all seen that famous still of her wearing a top hat and showgirl costume. I won't tell you any more of the story but there's no Hollywood happy ending – not even in the English version which was shot at the same time.'

'Wasn't there a remake a few years ago?' said Ivor who was also a keen filmgoer. Indeed, his knowledge of the cinema had impressed Sam who had been deep in reading some lengthy feature on film in the *Guardian* when Ivor had plucked up enough courage to approach her in Yummies Sandwich Bar.

'Clever boy,' she said admiringly. 'Yes, Curt Jurgens, May Britt and Theodore Bikel starred, Edward Dmytryk directed and Nigel Balchin wrote the script but updating the story didn't work at all.'

'And for £500, and I want the audience to be absolutely quiet here, no calling out, who composed the music and what was the name of the producer?' Ivor spoke in the quick-fire tones of a TV gameshow host as he thrust an imaginary microphone under Samantha's pretty little nose.

She shook her head and laughingly admitted: 'Sorry, Ivor, I'm afraid I haven't the faintest idea.'

'Tut-tut, my dear, that means you'll have to pay a forfeit later this evening,' drawled Ivor, wagging a warning finger.

'Oh, kind sir, please spare a poor girl,' begged Sam with a smile but her friend urged Ivor to stand firm. 'No, don't spare her, Ivor. Try and think of something slightly suitable,' said Katie with a wicked grin. 'So long as we can watch! But remember, you must not do anything in the street as we don't want to frighten the horses!'

'No problem, I'll dream up something if Ivor can't,' promised Martin as they reached the cinema. 'Perhaps we won't allow you to have a dessert at Roberto's after the film.'

'Roberto's in Sloane Street?' said Katie excitedly. 'Is that where we're going after the show? It's our favourite restaurant, isn't it, Sam? How wonderful – but even I couldn't be so cruel as not to let her choose something from the sweets trolley! Still, if I don't like the film I might change my mind!'

But in fact Sam's prediction about the others enjoying the film turned out to be quite accurate. All four walked back to the car in a jolly mood humming the song from the movie, *Falling in Love Again*, which catapulted Marlene Dietrich to international stardom. Yet again, fortune favoured Martin who managed to park just a few yards away from the chic Italian restaurant. He hadn't booked a table but the evening was going so well that he just knew he could ride his luck and they would be able to squeeze in, especially if he pressed some folding money into the hand of Cesare, the head waiter, who bustled up to them as they entered.

'*Buona sera*, Signor Reece, how nice to see you – you have a reservation?' asked Cesare and Martin shook his head. 'No, but I'm relying on you to queeze us in, Cesare,' murmured Martin, passing two pound notes to the plump little Italian.

'*Grazoe, ma è molto difficile*, Senor Reece, *Momento*, I see what I can do for you,' said the grateful waiter. As Martin had forecast, in less than ten minutes they were seated at one of the best tables and Cesare himself was taking their order. 'May I suggest tonight's speciality, *Agnello con piselli alla Toscana*, it is, how you say, roast leg of lamb with garlic and rosemary, tomatoes and oil with peas. It's very good tonight.'

'It is, how you say it,' laughed Martin, nudging Cesare in the ribs with his elbow. 'You were born in Naples but you've lived here since you were eight years old. So there's lots of lamb left over in the kitchen – what else is good?'

Cesare sighed and in his natural voice, that was far removed from Naples but which betrayed his upbringing in Neasden, said in an injured tone: 'Leave it out, Mr Reece, I wouldn't recommend anything that wasn't kosher. The lamb's really good but if anyone fancies a nice bit of fish, try the *Filetti di solgiola fantasia di Brida*.'

'M'mm, yes please, that's sole with shrimp shallots, and tomato with cream and artichokes isn't it?' said Katie, smacking her lips. 'If you like fish, Martin, I can recommend it.'

'No thanks, I fancy something simple. A plain *Escalope Milanese*, please, Cesare. Now how about you two?' asked Martin, for Ivor and Sam were still studying the menu. Ivor chose chicken and on Katie's recommendation Sam decided to order the sole. 'You can always get your teeth on something meaty later on,' whispered her friend, which made Sam giggle as Cesare asked them to choose their starters.

The meal was a great success and by the time the second bottle of Valpolicella had been emptied, the four of them were huddled together round the table exchanging the most intimate of confidences. The conversation had turned to embarrassing moments and Ivor had just recounted his story of how his love-making with Suzie had been interrupted at Billy Bucknall's birthday party. The girls exchanged glances when Ivor told them about how Tony Mulliken had joined in the fun and games and Martin said: 'I hope this tale hasn't given you the wrong idea about us. We don't make a habit of sharing our women!'

Sam shrugged her shoulders. 'No, I'm sure you don't, any more than we share our boy friends. But Katie and I don't have jealous natures and just occasionally a little threesome can be fun,' she said, tossing back her mane of blonde hair. 'I'll give you an example, if you like. About three months ago Katie and I were dating two American guys who were working over here on some Government scientific project at London University. Katie was going out with David and my boy friend's name was Louis. Well, one evening Katie was out of town and Louis called me to say that he and David had to attend some function or other at the American Embassy. It would be over by nine so would I like to see that new Antonioni film later at the Plaza?'

'*Blow Up*?' interrupted Ivor. 'I never got round to seeing it. Everyone's talking about that naughty bit when David Hemmings undresses a young model who has been pestering him to take photographs of her.'

'Yes, you and Martin will enjoy that scene. In fact we didn't see the film that night. I told Louis that I'd like to wait till Katie returned at the weekend and we could all go together. Instead, I suggested that they come round for a drink later that evening. Well, I had some supper and about nine o'clock decided to have a shower. I was now feeling tired and as it was getting late I thought the boys wouldn't come round so I put on a pair of panties and a thin see-through silk top and went to bed to read the copy of *Fanny Hill* which Katie had lent me. I thumbed through the pages and I must say that reading it did make me excited. It's such a saucy tale that I began to tingle all over as I imagined myself in Fanny's shoes, being screwed in all sorts of ways.

'It's just as well that I didn't wait up for the boys because it wasn't till almost eleven o'clock that there was a ring on the bell. My heart raced as I let them in and I could feel their eyes on my scantily clad body as I led them back to my bedroom and popped back between the sheets. They were very apologetic about being so late but the reception had gone on longer than planned. "And the worst news is that we're being recalled back home next week," said Louis sadly. "You and Sam will have to come over and see David and me in New York."

'"I'll put some coffee on, shall I?" suggested David and he went in the kitchen to put on the kettle. "I'll miss you," I said to Louis and he put his arm round me. "I'll miss you too, kid," he said as he sat down on the bed. I stretched across to him, exposing my breasts and nipples which were barely covered by the flimsy material of my top. "God, and how I will miss you!" he said thickly as I stroked the hard bulge which had sprung up in his lap. "Show me how much," I said softly and this made him growl with anticipation as he tore off his clothes and climbed into bed with me. He pulled me towards him and we began to French kiss, our tongues exploring each other's mouths as his hands roved all over my body. I wriggled my arms free out of my top so that his hands could cup my bare breasts. Then his hand moved down to peel my panties down my legs and I kicked them off. Louis' fingers then started to play around the moist hairs of my pussy and he slowly caressed my crotch. This made me open my legs to open my cunny and very soon his hand was doing wild things to my clitty that made me shiver all over.

'I took hold of his throbbing stiff cock and pulled his shaft faster and faster whilst he finger fucked me. We were threshing around so violently that the eiderdown fell to the floor and our naked bodies were totally exposed to David who came in just at this point with three cups of coffee on a tray. Although I saw his hands tremble, he managed to put the tray down on a table without spilling a drop. "Perhaps I'd better go and come back in again tomorrow," he joked but I told him to stay where he was.

'"Are you quite sure?" he asked shyly. Now keeping any kind of conversation going and preventing my body from twisting around whilst Louis was sliding his fingers in and out of my juicy pussy was impossible. The three of us fell silent and you could almost smell the sexual energy that was building up in the room as I moved my hand to touch the swelling erection in the front of his trousers. I could feel his prick pushing against the thin material of his trousers and I desperately wanted to see what he had to offer. Louis must have read my mind because he whispered: "Go on, Katie, unzip his fly and take it out." I breathed hard, pulled down the zip and pulled out

David's rock-hard boner. Like Louis he was circumcised but his shaft was one of those short, thick tools which I quite prefer to very big cocks which sometimes leave me sore after fucking.

'Anyhow, he stripped off in double quick time and jumped in to join us. We lay together in a beautiful lover's sandwich and a shiver went through me as I felt Louis's cock slide between my legs, neatly moving back and forth over my excited clitty whilst David's prick ran up against the crevice between my bum cheeks, hot and throbbing against my skin.

'We moved in unison as if it were the most natural thing in the world. I stroked both cocks, overcoming any remaining reservations I may have had. I rolled over, knelt over David and kissed his hot rod with my tongue and lips. Meanwhile Lous slid his face under my bum and his tongue darted straight into my cunt, licking and lapping so forcefully that it felt like a miniature cock was fucking me whilst I swirled my tongue around the mushroom knob of David's pulsating prick. I took him deep, to the hilt, into my throat and then sucked around the smooth, wet helmet as Louis brought me off to a tingling climax.

'Then David pulled his shaft from my mouth and moved to my side, stroking his tool and rubbing the crown against my erect nipple. Louis moved to my other side and directed his knob to my left tit. Lying there watching these two guys servicing their erect cocks on my breasts brought me to the brink of a second orgasm. My hand shot between my legs and I brought myself off again and again. Louis was now kissing my left boob whilst David continued to wank his knob against my tittie.

'It was all so exciting that I moaned for one of them to fuck me. I wanted a cock in my cunt so badly that it didn't matter whose tadger it was inside my cunny. I suppose I rather fancied trying David's thick prick but in fact it was Louis's blunt, fleshy knob which parted my pouting pussy lips, thrusting its way deep into my slithery, juicy hot love channel. With my eyes closed I lay there, fucking and being fucked, swaying my head from side to side. On one sway I felt the helmet of David'd cock on my lips and when I opened my eyes I saw his engorged knob in front of my face and I opened my mouth and swallowed it in.

'Louis pulled back his prick from my dripping honeypot long enough to roll me on my side facing him. He licked up some of David'd jism which had already leaked over my cheeks and then reinserted his veiny pole into my cunt. Now I felt an unbelievable new tingle as David's stiffie moved between my buttocks and I felt the wet tip of his knob nudge against my little bum hole. With slow, deep thrusts, Louis slewed his cock in and out of my sopping love box and as I relaxed, David shoved his knob inside my other hole. I let out a little scream of pained arousal but as we rocked together it soon felt better and smoother until we were all in an ecstatic union and I could feel both their cocks, their knobs separated only by a thin inner wall.

'David's movements became more rapid. The tight fit of my bum was too exciting for him and he stiffened, kissed me frantically on the neck, and squeezed my breasts before shooting his spunk into my burning back passage. He removed his still erect shaft from my bum and shifted himself round as Louis pulled his twitching tool from my cunny and moved round to that his cock was by my lips. As I took it inside my mouth David slid his cock inside my cunt and we continued until with a moan Louis jetted a river of sticky jism down my throat and David pumped a second fountain of sperm inside my pussy.

'Then the three of us collapsed in exhaustion, embracing, slick with sweat and love juice. Wow! What a night that was! But the bad news was that neither Katie nor I ever saw Louis Lempert or David Nash again as they had to fly back to New York even earlier than they thought. Still, we correspond and I'm keeping Louis' letters as he writes sheets of really colourful stuff about his screwing and I write back in the same vein.'

Ivor clucked his tongue against his cheek and said cheekily: 'Well then, it looks like I'll have to think up something special so you'll have something fresh to write about in your next letter.'

Martin called Cesare over and asked for the bill. When he returned Ivor dived into his pocket for his wallet but his boss waved him aside. 'No, this is on the firm,' he said generously. 'I don't see any reason as to why we can't put this down to entertaining foreign boys from America – what were their names again, Louis Lempert and David Nash, I'll just scribble a note to remind myself.'

'Now you know why he's the boss and I'm only an employee!' sighed Ivor as Martin wrote out a cheque and with a flourish presented it to Cesare.

'That was a lovely meal, Martin, thank you very much,' said Katie, giving him a kiss on his cheek. 'Now would you two boys like to have another coffee at our place?'

'Super,' said Ivor as they rose from the table and Cesare came over with their coats. 'It'll only take fifteen minutes to get back to Kilburn.'

It was approaching midnight and the streets had emptied out, but Martin was taking no chances after his earlier encounter with the law. It took almost half an hour before Martin drew up outside Sam and Katie's front door. 'Make sure you lock your doors,' advised Katie. 'The guy who lives downstairs had his car radio stolen last week.'

Martin nodded and checked the doors were locked as Sam fiddled in her bag for her key. Five minutes later the foursome had split up for no-one really wanted any further coffee. Sam and Ivor were locked into a passionate French kiss on the couch in the living room whilst in her bedroom, Katie was telling Martin softly to take off his shoes before joining her on the bed. Martin kicked off his moccasins as their mouths glued togeter in a frenzied kiss. But to his dismay Katie suddenly broke away – though she immediately soothed away his concern. 'Martin, don't start without me but I have to go to the loo.

27

I think that rich sauce over the sole is to blame. But I won't be too long,' she announced, giving his bulging erection a friendly rub as she heaved herself off the bed.

Meanwhile in the living room, Ivor and Sam were waggling their tongues together as Ivor fondled the soft breasts of the gorgeous girl. She wrapped her arms around him as he unhooked her dress at the neck and pulled down the zipper to let her free her arms from the sleeves. She unhooked her own brassiere and the garment fell away as her high, jutting breasts burst free, their engorged erect raspberry nipples already sticking out, just begging to be sucked. Sam slid out of her dress and lifted her pert little backside off the sofa so that Ivor cold pull down her tights and panties. He moved her arm downwards so that her hand lay on his stiff, throbbing truncheon.

'Wait, let me undress you,' whispered Sam as a high-pitched whimper escaped from Ivor's throat. She untied his tie and swiftly unbuttoned his shirt which he quickly discarded, at the same time stepping out of his shoes. Sam took off his socks and then kissed and nibbled his nipples, her mouth trailing down and into his navel as she unbuckled his belt and pulled off his trousers. His pulsating hard-on quivered upwards out of his boxer shorts and Sam gave his purple helmet a quick butterfly kiss before sliding them down over his buttocks and down over his legs. As soon as he was naked she crouched over him and grasped hold of his tool and swung the superb firm globes of her bottom over his face as she leaned forward and jammed her lips over his knob. The very sight of Sam's mass of blonde hair – it tickled the tops of his thighs whilst she sucked lustily on his trembling shaft – sent Ivor crazy with desire. He pulled her arse cheeks apart and wiggled the tip of his tongue all along the length of her wet slit. They indulged in fierce *soixante neuf* before Sam lifted her lips from his cock and in a steady voice said: 'I want to be fucked now, Ivor.'

He let his head fall backwards and Sam pulled down a

cushion from the couch and settled her head against it as she lay on her back on the carpet. Ivor slid down and knelt between her legs and she pulled his head to her breasts which he kissed passionately, turning his head from side to side, nibbling each raised nipple in turn. Then Ivor reached down and set his hand directly onto her bushy mound as he raised his face to hers. Their lips met whilst his fingers splayed themselves in her silky blonde thatch through which he could feel the moist pussy lips and raised clitty which twitched under his fingertip. Sam gasped as Ivor dexterously parted the rolled pink lips of her cunny and, ever so lightly, traced the wet, open crack of her cunt with his fingers, flicking her excited tiny clitty that was now protruding out of her love channel.

As he continued to suck on her horned-up nipples Sam threw back her head and wailed with unslaked desire. A wide smile broke out on Ivor's face as the trembling girl lay back, opened her legs and pulled his straining shaft towards the warm, wet haven which awaited it. He climbed on his knees between her parted thighs and took hold of his gleaming prick, easing in the wide purple crown between the pouting lips of Sam's juicy pussy, propelling it in inch by inch until their pubic hairs were matted, his black and her blonde curls making a contrasting pattern as they mingled together.

Ivor pulled all but the knob of his cock out of her clinging honeypot and then drove the full length of his rod fully inside the lovely girl, again and again as she urged him on. Sam swung her long legs over his back and her heels drummed against his spine to force even more of his pulsating staff inside her. He grasped the cheeks of her bottom and pulled her even more tightly against his muscular body as he plunged his glistening cock with increasing speed in and out of her squishy slit.

'Yes, yes, yes, slide your cock in, darling!' Sam gasped as her body rocked in rhythm with Ivor's powerful thrusts. 'I'm going to come, Ivor!' Shoot your spunk into me! Come on, you randy fucker!'

This triggered Ivor's own orgasm and with a hoarse cry he rammed home his twitching tool and unleashed a flood of frothy white jism into her already squelchy cunt. Sam groaned and shuddered as rivulets of Ivor's spunk and her own love juices overflowed out of her pussy and dribbled down her thigh. They clasped their arms round each other, exhausted.

As Ivor and Sam recovered from their magnificent if exhausting fuck, Katie came padding back into her bedroom, clad only in a silk wrapround bathrobe. She looked down at Martin and said: 'Sorry to have left you, but now I'm more than ready – but, hey, why haven't you undressed?'

Martin blushed and quickly began to tear at the buttons of his shirt. 'I didn't want to presume that you wanted to fuck,' he murmured. 'And anyhow, some girls like to undress their men.'

'That's very considerate of you,' said Katie, sitting on the bed and stretching out her hand to rub her palm against his rigid rod. 'It's true that many girls do like to undress their boys but, if anything, I prefer to have a man undress me – no, don't worry, I'm not going to put my clothes back on just to have you take them all off again! But I certainly do like to be played with while we're necking and I love to feel my blouse being unbuttoned and being fondled all over before having my panties pulled down.'

'I'm sure we can arrange something,' said Martin thickly as Katie unzipped his fly and he wriggled his legs out of his trousers as he freed his arms from his shirt. Katie slid the robe off her shoulders and lay beside him, both naked now except for her skimpy pink panties and his white Y-fronts through which his cock bulged dangerously, with the very tip of his rosy knob peeking over the elasticated top.

They hugged and rubbed against each each and Katie wiggled her bum as Martin slipped his hand inside her knickers and squeezed her jingling buttocks before effortlessly despatching her panties down over her legs until they reached her ankles. Katie kicked them off and returned the compliment, tugging down his pants while Martin's stiff shaft sprang up to greet her. She licked her lips as she gripped it in both hands, pulling down his foreskin to bare the purple rounded crown from which she licked away the first drops of pre-come juice. Then she lifted her face and they kissed while she continued to manipulate his palpitating prick as he caressed the creamy white globes of her full, rounded breasts. He rolled his palms on her elongated nipples and then his head fell to lick and suck her hard red cherry titties and he let one hand fall to roam around her curly triangle of pussy hair around her dampening crack.

'I want to ride you, lover,' she whispered into his ear. 'Just lie there and let me do all the work.'

'Be my guest,' replied Martin and settled himself down. As Katie sat astride him and placed his knob between the lips of her now thoroughly wet pussy, he added lewdly: 'Feel my balls, Katie, they feel so heavy they must be overflowing with the jism I'm going to shoot inside your juicy little love box.'

Then very slowly and deliberately she began to slide her love channel down upon his yearning penis until she had taken every last inch of its length down to the root inside her cunt. 'A-a-a-h!' she sighed as she thrilled to the feel of Martin's sturdy, velvet-skinned cock. Her cunny muscles were contracting and expanding, gripping and releasing in the most heavenly way for them both as Katie bounced up and down his rigid rod at an ever-increasing speed. Soon this fucking sparked off a sharp series of crackling comes for Katie which racked through her body as she flung herself up and down on Martin's pulsating penis.

This uninhibited love-making delighted Martin and he clutched Katie's bum cheeks as she leaned forward to let the edge of his knob rub against her clitty. She began to push up and down again, squeezing his thighs with her knees. Soon she felt his shaft filling up with spunk as, with a groan, he jetted a sticky fountain of spunk inside her engorged cunt. Her own juices mingled as she now sat still on his twitching tool, watching the gooey liquid seep down from her pussy.

At once she rolled off and propped herself up on one elbow, watching Martin's face as she traced delicate patterns with her fingernail on his flaccid juice-coated shaft. He opened his eyes and gave a tiny smile.

'Sorry if I came too soon, Katie,' he said apologetically. 'But that was the most wonderful fuck that I just couldn't hold on any longer.'

'That's all right, Martin, boys always shoot up the ladder quicker than girls and the earth doesn't have to move every time,' said Katie soothingly. 'Most men have to grit their teeth and hold on and every guy has his own way of prolonging a fuck. For example, take my American guy, David Nash – he sometimes tried to recite the Prologue to Shakespeare's *Henry V* just to keep his cock from spurting and this usually worked. It doesn't sound romantic, does it? But of course I was grateful that he was being a kind and considerate lover.'

Martin relaxed and soon he and Katie joined the other couple, who had moved into Sam's bedroom, in the land of Nod. Ivor was the first to stir as the early rays of dawn filtered through the curtains. He looked down at his rock-hard cock which was poking against Sam's soft buttock. He had recently discovered that the majority of men wake up with a boner that is caused by the rise of the male hormone testosterone. Ivor felt just a little cheated, as he had always thought that only well-hung randy studs like himself started the day with a huge, throbbing erection.

Was Sam ready for an early morning joust, he wondered as he slid his arm across her and fondled her nipples? She purred contentedly and squeezed his shaft as she rolled over onto her back and lay there with her eyes closed but with a wicked little smile playing sensously across her lips. Sam looked truly beautiful with the long tresses of blonde hair falling suggestively over her shoulders and onto her pointed breasts. She stretched and arched her back, moving her legs suggestively as Ivor covered her face with kisses as he placed his hand on the silky blonde mossy growth between her legs. He commenced his love-making by planting a pattern of quick kisses on her creamy thighs and then he teased his tongue around the damp pubic bush whilst running his forefinger all along her damp crack. Her soft body twisted lasciviously as his thumb found her clitty and she grabbed his hair and pushed his head into her golden thatch. 'Oh Ivor, eat me!' she sighed and he looked up and blew her a kiss before licking his lips and running his tongue lower through the crinkly cunny hair. His hands encircled her firm, rounded bum cheeks as he buried his head between her thighs. Sam gurgled with delight as Ivor's tongue inserted itself between her pussy lips and he began licking and lapping at her juicy honeypot, sucking up her tangy love juices as her pussy writhed against his mouth.

After a minute or so of this exquisite stimulation of her pussy, Sam breathed: 'Ivor, I'm ready for you!' and so he heaved himself over her and let the beautiful blonde guide his stiffstander straight into her cunt. He slid his prick in and very slowly pulled in and out, creating a huge suction in Sam's love channel. She was getting more and more excited especially when he reached under her and put his fingertip directly into her bum-hole and gently rubbed around the rim of the wrinkled little rosette. At first Sam tensed up but then soon started to enjoy the new sensation. Ivor rammed his cock harder and faster into her cunt whilst at the same time his finger pushed in about quarter of an inch inside her arse-hole. His finger and cock worked simultaneously and then alternately; whilst his shaft was all the way inside her cunt he withdrew his finger from her bum and then, just as he withdrew his thick prick from her cunt, he would plunge his finger in up to the first knuckle.

'Yes, yes, YES!' Sam screamed as she exploded into a mighty orgasm. Her infectious excitement stimulated

Ivor into spurting spasm after spasm of hot jism inside her welcoming cunny.

They lay sated whilst in the next room the other pair slept on. 'I'd better wake Martin up soon,' said Ivor regretfully. 'He has to be back home at a reasonable time.'

'Why? In case his wife rings him?' asked Sam, and, as Ivor bit his lip, she added hastily. 'Oh, come on, don't look so worried, Katie and I guessed that Martin was married – not that we had to be that clever to see the white band round his finger where he'd taken off his wedding ring.'

Ivor looked gloomily at the floor as Sam continued: 'It's alright, Katie knows the score – she fancied Martin and knows that it's strictly a one-night stand. She doesn't want any commitment right now because between you and me she's really keen on this American guy David Nash. She's hoping he'll ask her to go and live with him in New York but meanwhile she's only human and likes a good fuck now and then.'

'And how about you, Samantha Garrett? Is there a future for you and me? For my part, I'd very much like to see you again,' said Ivor softly.

Sam bit her lip and thought for a moment before replying: I've very much enjoyed this evening, Ivor, and I want you to know that I don't make a habit of fucking with every man who takes me out, especially on the first date. But I have to be honest about my feelings. The fact of the matter is that I'm just getting over a really intense love affair and I'm just not in the frame of mind to begin a new relationship just now. So can we leave things open for a couple of weeks? You've got my telephone number, haven't you? Please don't throw it away but promise you'll call me early next month.'

'Fair enough,' said Ivor gloomily. 'I'll phone you without fail.' But this conversation had left them both feeling slightly jaded and though they showered together, neither felt sexy as the jets of warm water sluiced across their naked bodies. However, there was little time to ponder further as when Ivor knocked on Katie's door he heard Martin yawn and then let out an oath as he looked at his watch. 'Christ, is that the time? I must be getting along pronto.'

❊ TWO ❊

Sunday, Sunday

Ten minutes later the boys were waving goodbye to Sam and Katie from inside Martin's Jaguar as he pulled away quickly from the kerb. 'Two nice girls, weren't they?' remarked Martin contentedly. 'And last night certainly made up for an awful lot of previous aggravation last week! Do you plan to see Samantha again?'

'I'd very much like to, but I'm not sure whether she'll be interested,' said Ivor with a slight edge of sadness in his voice. 'Martin, you do realise we were just one night stands as far as Sam and Katie were concerned? Now that might be very convenient for you but I wouldn't have minded getting to know Sam a little better.'

'Christ, from the sounds I heard coming out of her bedroom I would have thought you got to know her pretty well last night!'

'In one way perhaps, but there's more than sex in a good relationship.'

Martin gave a short laugh and said: 'You sound like one of those agony aunts in the women's magazines. Anyhow, you may be right that there are other important matters in a friendship. Sex *is* very important if you're going to progress from first base with any girl because neither you nor any girl you meet will ever be happy if you both can't romp around in bed.'

And with that dictum, Martin swung his car neatly into a parking space and switched off the engine. 'I'd better be getting in, as Sheila will be back in about an hour. If by any chance you see her in the office next week, remember we went for a walk on the Heath this morning.'

'Sure, Martin, see you tomorrow,' said Ivor as he lifted himself out of the car. 'I have to be in early for that meeting you set up with that fellow from Sunbronze suntan tablets. What's his name again?'

'Mark Hamilton. You'll like him, Ivor, he's a nice guy, sharp but on the level. Remember, I'll just bring him into the boardroom and it'll be up to you to convince him that Cable Publicity should handle his public relations.'

'Leave it to me,' said Ivor as he took a deep breath of the fresh Spring air. 'I think I will actually go and take a walk on the Heath. Oh, if Sheila doesn't come back till later, I'm taking Sheena for a curry at the Taj Mahal in Hampstead High Street. You're very welcome to join us if you find yourself at a loose end.'

Sheena Shackleton was Ivor's former secretary. She had been tempted away from her job by the offer to work as personal assistant to the showbiz impressario and agent Bob Maxwell, the man who discovered Ruff Trayde and a host of pop stars. Whilst he was sorry to lose Sheena's services, at least her appointment meant that Ivor had a friend in court although these days he only supervised Ruff Trayde's publicity, leaving the day-to-day work to his account executives. At first Ivor missed Sheena's orderly, efficient way of running his office. Her replacement, Juliette Burillo, had never worked in a public relations agency before, but his new secretary was a pretty and intelligent girl, sophisticated, quick-tongued and the dark, flashing eyes Juliette had inherited from her Spanish father had captivated most of the men who worked at Cable Publicity. And as Ivor had soon noticed, her smouldering good looks also brought his new assistant to the admiring attention of several clients as well.

'Thanks, but I'm not sure Sheila will be back before lunch. We're supposed to join Harry Godfrey and his wife for drinks at around twelve. Still, after that great fuck last night, I'll be able to listen to him crowing about Spurs hammering Fulham without getting too riled up! See you tomorow, mate.'

38

Ivor drove home and changed into jeans and a red sweater before driving up to Hampstead Heath where he bought a *Sunday Mirror* and sat down on a bench to read a report of the game he and Martin had watched the previous afternoon. 'Hi, Ivor,' said a cheery voice from behind his left shoulder. 'I wouldn't have thought you wanted to look at the sports pages this morning.'

He looked up to see his cousin, Keith Barnes, standing at his side. Keith was a qualified doctor of medicine but he had given up general practice to take up a lucrative research post with an international drugs company. Ivor never quite understood what work Jonathan actually did but his cousin was always flying off to conferences in Europe and America and having a great time, wining and dining fellow medical men and women at his company's expense all over the world.

'Poor old Fulham,' continued his cousin with a grin. 'Never mind, I hear they're about to sign a fabulous new player from Hong Kong.'

'Really?' said Ivor, taking the bait.

'Sure, a fellow by the name of Wee Wun Wunce,' chuckled Dr Barnes. 'Ivor, you must be a bloody masochist to follow Fulham. You don't like being whipped by your girl friends, I suppose?'

Ivor shook his head. 'No, not my scene at all. You dating at all these days, Keith?'

'Well, I still see quite a lot of Maureen but I'm away so much that it's never got very serious,' said Dr Barnes, sitting himself down besides Ivor. 'Here, I had a great time at a heart disease conference in Dallas last week. The Americans had decided to house all the foreign delegates in a brand new swanky hotel which should have been all fine and dandy – but the builders had rushed to open the hotel on time and the air-conditioning hadn't been properly installed. It went on the blink almost as soon as we arrived and it was damnably hot in my suite, I can tell you.

'Anyhow, I'd unpacked and taken a shower and I was sitting stark naked in an armchair making notes for the talk I had to give the next day, when all of a sudden the door swings open and in walks a lovely coloured maid carrying a tray with a bottle of champagne in an ice-bucket. I don't know who was more surprised when she came in but I hastily covered myself as best I could with my notebook as she looked at me with a horrified expression on her face. "Oh my, I am so sorry, sir, I thought the room was unoccupied," she blurted out but of course I was only shocked and not in the least annoyed. I looked at the girl who was very attractive, slim with long, bare legs. All she wore was a tight pink cotton mini-dress and her breasts pushed up against the material so firmly that I could clearly see from the way the dark nipples stood out she was not wearing any bra.

'"Don't worry, anyone can make a mistake," I said, rising up from my chair. I backed across to the bed where I turned round, flashing my bare backside at her whilst I slipped on a bathrobe. "My name is Carrie, sir, from room service. Call me any time if there's anything you need," she said. As I looked over her supple body she asked shyly: "Are you one of the doctors from England, sir? I hope you'll be very comfortable here. The champagne is with the hotel's compliments. The mechanics are here right now and we hope to have the air-conditioning working by this evening."

'Well, I'll cut a long story short and just tell you that I managed to persuade her to come back to my room when she'd finished putting the bottles of champagne out in all the other rooms on the eighteenth floor. After all, I said, I couldn't manage to drink a whole bottle of bubbly by myself! Anyway, she sat down and we watched TV whilst we polished off the booze and Carrie told me that she was only a part-time maid and was really a student working her way through college. As time went by I began to move closer and closer to her until her lithe, sexy body was nestling in my arms. She was sitting in such a way that her dress kept riding up and exposing her tiny white panties. At first she'd pull the hem of her dress down but after a while she let it slide up higher and higher.

'She caught me looking at her crotch just as I noticed a dark, damp spot there. Her wide eyes casually travelled to the bulge in my lap as I pulled her towards me and we kissed. I cupped her left breast in my hand and she reached down between the folds of my robe and slid her fingers around my aching cock. Her eyes grew wide as her hand slipped up and down my shaft and then she sat back up and pulled her dress off over her head whilst I shucked off my robe. She stood in front of me as I carefully pulled down her panties to reveal the prettiest little pussy you could ever want to see, with just a tiny triangle of curly black hair above her lips.

'Now I stood up and we kissed again, our bodies pressed together with just my bulging stiffie between us! We reeled drunkenly towards the bed where she made me lay on my back as she kissed my nipples before lowering her head to let her tongue tickle my helmet. Then she opened her mouth and took in inch after inch of my tadger until her nose was rubbing against my balls. God, it was exciting as her tongue moved around, rubbing here, massaging there and generally making my prick feel very happy indeed. I don't know how Carrie knew, but each time I was about to spunk she left off her slippery sucking to let my wet shaft quiver like a flagpole in the breeze.

'Finally, Carrie climbed on top of me with her knees on either side. She pulled open her cunny lips with her fingers and began to rub her pussy across the tip of my knob. Then she guided my cock home, slowly tightening the walls of her cunt to hold me in place. Then she started to ride me, twisting her hips and bumping and grinding away with my prick jammed inside her sopping cunt. I grasped hold of her sleek black body and pulled her down so that her large dark nipples were against my lips. When I began to suck and nibble on them she really went wild, thrashing around like a mad woman, rocking backwards and forwards as she climaxed just when I gave a great push upwards and shot my load up into her juicy puss.'

'Phew, she sounds better than any medicine you've ever prescribed, you jammy bugger,' said Ivor wistfully. He had never screwed a black girl and he was even keener to fulfil this ambition having listened to his cousin's lascivious tale.

'I dare say, but that's not the end of the story. I was feeling flat out after drinking more than half a bottle of champagne and then being sucked off, but Carrie wanted me to fuck her again straighaway!'

'Blimey, was your old man up to it, Keith?'

Dr Barnes wiped his brow at the remembrance of the moment. 'Not right then, Ivor, leave it out, I'm not superman. After all, I'll be thirty three next month and I dare say neither of us can fuck all night like we could fifteen years ago! No, I played for time by changing positions with her except that I buried my face as opposed to my cock between her legs. "Oooh, that's lovely," she cooed as I planted my lips against her dripping crack. "I adore having my pussy eaten."

'"Good show, I've been awarded a black belt in cunnilingus," I mumbled as I dived down to begin munching her muff. Her legs trembled as I parted her swollen cunt lips with my fingertips. I sniffed the clean sweet scent of pussy which wafted up my nose. I slid one hand under her bouncy bum cheeks for elevation and with the other I spread her pussy lips with my thumb and middle finger. I placed my lips over her still erect clitty and gobbled it into my mouth, feeling it expand as her legs began to jerk up and down as I tongue-fucked her. Her juices flowed freely as I lapped away inside her cunt and I could feel her cunny muscles spasming around my tongue, especially when I found the little button under the fold at the base of the clitty. The faster I vibrated my tongue around it, the more she began to moan and by now I was almost drowning in her love juice as, with each stroke, she arched her body up in ecstacy, pressing her clitty up against my mouth.

'Suddenly she tensed and screamed out: "I'm coming! Oh God, I'm coming!" and I felt her explode as I gulped down the gush of pussy juice which came flooding out of her as she climaxed.

'Now I thought that this would satisfy her, but young Carrie was insatiable. "Keith, I want your cock inside my honeypot again. Is it ready yet?" she implored. Well, thank goodness, I'd somehow managed to recover my strength but my tool was not totally stiff so she squirmed down the bed and sucked my knob into her mouth. She rolled her lips over the top before washing it all over with her tongue and now I was more than ready for the fray.

'This time I climaxed on top as Carrie grasped my rock-hard prick and placed it between her thighs just at the entrance of her sopping slit. I pushed forward an inch or so which made her giggle with delight as I teased her cunny lips before plunging fully into her hot, wet cave. I began my thrusts slowly but then worked up to a faster rhythm. She squealed as I thrust to and fro, lifting her bum to meet me as her own hands massaged my bollocks. I pounded into her pussy like a man possessed, my balls slapping against her bum as, with a final wrenching heave, I squirted a second torrent of spunk inside her and she arched her back to take in the gushes of jism that were shooting out of my knob.

'I wanted Carrie to stay for the rest of the evening but she had to get dressed and finish her work and I never managed to get to grips with her again. But if I ever have to go to Dallas again, I certainly know in which hotel to stay! Carrie was the best screw I've had this year though the girl at the reception desk at the Ossulton Hotel in Brussels must come a close second.'

'It's all right for you jet-setters, fucking yourselves silly in all these posh hotels,' complained Ivor. 'If there's any justice left in this wicked world, your prick will fall off one day through over-use.'

'Sorry, Ivor, all the evidence shows that to the contrary, screwing keeps you healthy. You know the old saying – a good fuck a day keeps the doctor away?'

'Surely you mean an apple a day?'

Dr Barnes tut-tutted and slapped his cheek. 'Oh dear, is it really? Then I've been getting it wrong for some time now! Still, it doesn't seem to have done me any harm!' he guffawed as he rose up and patted Ivor on the shoulder. 'See you soon, cousin, why not give me a ring later in the week and we'll have a drink somewhere. I wouldn't mind going to that Hunkiedorie Club you told me about. Must dash now, though, I'm having an early Sunday lunch with Mum and Dad as I'm driving up to Leeds this afternoon. I'll be back in town by Wednesday afternoon.'

'Give them my love,' called Ivor as his cousin moved smartly along the path to the car park. He looked at his watch and decided that he might as well stroll back to his car and drive down to Hampstead High Street where he could sink a lager in The Flask pub before meeting Sheena in the restaurant.

One of his former secretary's most endearing traits had been her unfailing punctuality and as he was now feeling quite peckish, Ivor was delighted to see Sheena Shackleton enter the Taj Mahal just a couple of minutes after one o'clock. He stood up to greet her and they exchanged a warm hug and kiss as the waiter skilfully relieved Sheena of her fawn raincoat. Ivor appraised the attractive long legged girl who was brushing away a stray lock of blonde hair from her eyes. 'Sheena, you're looking great – working for Bob Maxwell must really agree with you. All the papers say he's the toughest of the tough in a cut-throat business but obviously you're thriving on it. I can see there's no chance of your ever coming back to the old firm and helping me out of all the scrapes I seem to get myself into.'

'No chance, Ivor, I love the music business,' she replied, taking the proferred menu from the waiter. 'It's a ruthless world and a bit shady round the edges, if you ask me, but we work hard and play hard.'

'Yes, I've heard that Bob Maxwell's good at both,' joked Ivor. 'Now, what do you fancy?'

Over their meal they drank a bottle of surprisingly good, cheap white wine and afterwards, as they sipped their coffee, Sheena asked Ivor if he would like to see her new flat in nearby Belsize Park. 'I only moved in last week and it's still in a bit of a mess. But it's so convenient as I'm near the Underground and as Bob's moved his office to Oxford Street, I'm less than half an hour away. We can open a bottle of Courvoisier that Ruff Trayde's record producer gave me as a flat-warming present.'

'Sure, thank you,' said Ivor as he slid a couple of pound notes on the plate where the bill had been placed. As they walked hand in hand over to his car, a sharp pang of regret racked through Ivor's mind that he had never tried to be more than just a boss to Sheena. He had always believed in the old maxim that you should never mix business with pleasure. Probably any affair would have led to complications but, as he shot a swift glance at his former secretary's sleek, lissome looks, Ivor told himself that he had been crazy not even to have attempted to find out whether any amorous attentions would have been welcomed.

Ah well, perhaps it was just as well, reflected Ivor as they drove the short distance down Haverstock Hill to Belsize Park. Once in Sheena's high ceilinged apartment, Ivor helped tidy away some of the debris as neither Sheena nor Debbie, her flat-mate, had fully unpacked all their bits and pieces. 'Debbie's gone down to Eastbourne to visit her parents this weekend. She won't be back till tonight,' said Sheena as she rummaged around in the cupboard before triumphantly bringing out two balloon-shaped brandy glasses. They flopped down onto two blue bean bags and Sheena poured two large measures of Courvoisier.

45

'Well, at lunch you told me about who's been having whom at the office,' said Sheena, settling herself down into the soft contours of the bean bag. 'Now how about you, Ivor? Are you going steady yet, or are you still screwing anything in a skirt?'

'Leave it out, I don't go for every girl who crosses my path!' But Sheena would have none of it. 'Come on, you've had more girls than I've had hot dinners.'

'Not so, love – why, we never made it together, did we?'

'*Touché*, Ivor, but I don't count as we were working together and we both knew that getting together after hours would have been courting disaster.'

Ivor gave her an evil grin. 'Well, we're not business colleagues any more. How about making up for lost time?'

She giggled and held up her hand. 'No, I don't think so. Have some more brandy instead. To be honest with you, right now my love life has been pretty dormant for the last couple of weeks.'

'Dormant?' A super chick like you?' said Ivor stoutly. 'I simply cannot believe there isn't a queue of fellows waiting to knock on your door.'

Sheena sighed and took a deep swig from her glass. 'Thank you, kind sir. I suppose there are two or three guys who ring me up every so often to ask me out but at the moment I'm not sure I want to get involved.'

'Why ever not? 'Tis better to have loved and lost than never to have loved at all – and all that jazz. Has some nasty experience put you off men?' He moved himself round to hold her hand as Sheena settled her head into his shoulder.

'You're not just a pretty face, are you,' smiled Sheena ruefully. 'That's exactly, well, almost exactly the situation. I'll tell you what happened but in strict confidence. I don't want Martin or anyone in your office or mine to know about it.'

'Word of honour,' promised Ivor, now moving his arm round her shoulders. 'I won't tell a living soul.'

'Okay, I trust you. Well, it all started three weeks ago when your photographer pal Brian Lipman persuaded me to go out with him on a shoot for *Ram*,' said Sheena, snuggling even closer into his body.

'*Ram*? The glossy men's magazine with naughty photographs?'

'Yes, but the photographs are beautifully done, lovely lighting, colour, the works,' said Sheena defensively. Ivor immediately remembered how once, when he had been searching for a file in one of her desk drawers, he had seen a set of photographs Brian Lipman had taken of Sheena. She had looked tremendously sexy, seated on a sofa with her feet propped up on a coffee table, naked except for a tiny white pair of bikini panties, with her long blonde hair swept up and pinned and she was smiling seductively at the camera. Another print had shown her with the panties discarded, though her hands were strategically placed between her legs. He had then just had time to peek at the next photographs which showed her fluffy blonde pussy when Sheena had returned to the office and he had hastily returned the photographs to the drawer.

'Have the photographs been published yet? If not, I'll tell my newsagent to reserve me twenty copies of *Ram* so I can give them to friends as birthday presents,' joked Ivor.

'I didn't think you had so many friends!' rejoined Sheena with a giggle. 'Anyhow, Brian told me they'll be used in the magazine's November issue.'

'I'll make a note of it – after all it's not every day that your former secretary makes a clean breast of it!'

Sheena burst out laughing and shook her head. 'Bad luck, Ivor, I'm sorry to disappoint you but Brian Lipman just asked me along for the ride. He said that sometimes the presence of another girl helped the model to relax and as he had booked Janice, a new but expensive teenage girl, he wanted to take as many shots as possible not only for *Ram* but for American and European glamour magazines. So I'm afraid that I stayed well behind the camera!'

'Oh,' said Ivor glumly. 'Well, I'm sure you would have looked just as if not more alluring than the model.'

'Flattery will get you everywhere, kind sir! But to come back to what I was saying before, it was Janice that actually triggered the whole business which made me act in a way I never thought possible. Brian had picked her up from Swiss Cottage station before calling for me. When I first saw Janice sitting in the back of Brian's car I could immediately see why he had paid over the odds for her services. She was a real head-turner. If anything she looked younger than her age, with masses of dark hair and blue eyes, a tip-tilted nose and a wide, full mouth. She was wearing a low-cut baby blue angora sweater which showed her huge breasts to good advantage and I doubted whether she was wearing any bra underneath. She had good legs too which were crossed and her white skirt had ridden right up over her thighs.

'Janice was a friendly girl and we sat chatting away in the car whilst Brian drove us to Bricket Wood in Hertfordshire where he had found a secluded country setting which he wanted to use for the shots. We were lucky with the weather as it had rained earlier on but now the sun was shining and Brian said he would be able to use one of these new ultra-fast films so would be able to dispense with his flash. He was able to park on a narrow stone path and we only had to walk through fifty yards of wood before we came to an open glade. "This is it, girls. I think the green and brown from the trees and shrubs will make a marvellous backdrop for us," said Brian as he began setting up a tripod and loading his camera.

'I asked Janice if I could help her prepare in any way. "Thanks, I'll probably ask you to give my make-up the final once-over," she said gratefully as she pulled the sweater up over her head.

'My earlier thought about her lack of underwear was proved correct when she started to undress – indeed, Janice wasn't even wearing a slip let alone a bra and her gorgeous bare breasts crowned with large tawney tittles jiggled sexily in the bright mid-morning light. Then she unzipped her skirt and stepped out of it to reveal a pair of lace-front string bikini panties with a heart shaped cotton panel which cutely covered her pussy. She was wearing high-heeled, ankle-strapped shoes which emphasised the curves of her legs. Later, she told me that most model girls wore high-heeled shoes as they lift your bottom nicely though I couldn't tell that as she sat on the floor of Brian's car with her legs outside on the ground, checking her mascara and lipstick in the mirror. I helped Janice brush her long silky hair which she wore in a simple fashion with an off centre parting and letting the dark strands fall naturally over her ears and down to her shoulders.

'Brian began to work straightaway and concentrated mostly on her face and upper body at first. But then she slipped her knickers down along her elegant long legs and stepped out of them. I could see Brian catching his breath and smiling as she passed her hand across the curly black thatch that nestled over her cunt. Though I could see a bulge form in his jeans, he's a true professional and he continued to snap away from all angles. Yes, Brian must have used four or five rolls of film, making the girl sit, stand, and lie down in all sorts of weird and wonderful poses.

'We made a bed of leaves for Janice and she lay with her back up against a tree, her legs open and her pink little pussy lips were pouting out of that bush of black curls. I could just visualise Brian Lipman getting on his knees, his hands on her thighs, licking and lapping her hairy cunt, making her body squirm as she played with her erect tawney nipples, rubbing them up until they were as hard as two little brown bullets.

'At about half past twelve Brian could see that Janice was getting tired and said we should take a break for lunch. After she had dressed herself we walked back to the car and he added; "I thought we'd have a bite of lunch

49

at the house of a friend of mine who lives in Radlett village. It's only about three miles away. Warren's a merchant banker and he's in Paris for a couple of days on business but he's left me the keys of his house and there'll be plenty of food in the fridge."

'I suppose we shouldn't really have opened that second bottle of Chardonnay with our cheese and cucumber sandwiches but we did and not surprisingly we needed a little nap after lunch. So Janice and I went upstairs and lay down on the bed together whilst Brian said he would put his feet up on the sofa.

'"It's so lovely and warm, let's make ourselves really comfortable and take all our clothes off," suggested Janice. "What a good idea," I said and we stripped off and lay naked together on the crisp linen sheets. I was genuinely tired and soon my eyes were fluttering and I must have dozed off quite quickly. But I wasn't deeply asleep and shortly afterwards I imagined that soft lips were brushing against my bare breast – and then opening wide to engulf a nipple which was then washed all over by a soft, wet tongue. I was shocked but even the mere thought of resistance was wrenched from my mind when that same tongue started to flick against my now erect nipple. I said nothing when Janice placed her fingers around my other tittie and began to roll it around her palm until it stiffened up like a miniature prick.

'She then placed her hand on my moistenig notch and massaged the insides of my thighs. Soon I felt quite light-headed as she now made love to me quite uninhibitedly, kissing and sucking my breasts, frigging my pussy and squeezing and pinching my bum. I made no attempt to stop her when she eased a forefinger into my dampening crack and I let out little yelps of satisfaction when she finger fucked me at an increasing pace.

'We were writhing around on the bed so intent on pleasuring ourselves that we did not hear Brian Lipman come in, let alone see him take his clothes off! The first I knew of his presence was when he cleared his throat and said? "Now look here, girls, we've got work to do and there's something I want to get straight."

'"So do I!" said Janice with a dirty laugh, and she took hold of his swollen circumcised cock and gobbled his knob straight into her mouth.

'As you might have guessed, we stayed in Radlett for longer than we should have done. I hadn't taken part in a threesome for some time and I enjoyed it very much.'

Ivor gave her a long, lascivious look as he remarked: 'I've been in a few *menage à trois* scenes myself, Sheena. I think they're best with one man and two women.

'Oh yes, you're right,' she agreed. 'The most exciting moment was when we were all naked with Janice lying on top of me, our tummies and breasts pressed together while her legs stretched out over mine. Brian moved between her legs and, after he had pulled her up to him, pushed his pole between the crevice of her bum into her pussy doggie-style. As he fucked her she moaned and kissed my lips and nipples and when his pumping brought her near to a climax she grabbed my breasts and squeezed them hard.

'Then Janice pulled one leg over mine and pushed her thigh up against my cunt. We were both soaking with love juice as she climbed up and thrust her hairy minge in my face. I buried my face in the soft dark curls and began to lick out her cunt, probing her slit gently with my tongue. I grasped her bum cheeks to hold her still as she began to toss from side to side.

'Behind her Brian Lipman slipped a pillow underneath her bottom and slid his throbbing wet cock into my own dripping pussy. It all added up to one of the most exciting sensations I have ever had – I brought Janice off with my tongue just as Brian shot a fierce gush of spunk into my lovebox. He continued to work his cock inside my lathered sheath until I shuddered into a tremendous orgasm.

'We stayed for two hours, finding some wonderful new positions and we never got back to Bricket Wood, as

Brian decided to finish his work in the house. He took some saucy photos of the three of us using his time exposure device.'

'I'd love to see those photographs,' said Ivor, squeezing Sheena's body even closer to him. 'I'm sure Brian must have sent you a set of proofs.'

'Of course he did and he even gave me the negatives as he didn't want me to worry where they might end up. Wasn't that nice of him?' said Sheena. Ivor decided not to disillusion the girl although he would have bet a thousand pounds that Brian Lipman had already mailed duplicate negatives of the best sizzling shots to his agents in New York and Amsterdam.

Instead he said quietly: 'Aren't I pretty nice too?' and kissed her on her rich, red lips. She responded and murmured: 'Oh, Ivor, is this a clever thing to do?'

'I don't see why not,' he rejoined as he kissed her eyes, her cheeks and her little nose in quick succession. 'We're no longer working together in the same office.'

'But we're still involved in business meetings,' objected Sheena, although she made no resistance as Ivor's lips covered her own and covered them with with a passionate kiss. Their faces pressed closer together and their tongues slid wetly around inside each other's mouths. Emboldened now Ivor unfastened the buttons on her blouse and cupped her firm rounded breasts, pinching the nipples and squeezing the soft globes. Sheena's hand strayed down to his lap and he helped her unzip his trousers. She plunged her hand inside and grasped his hard, vibrant cock which sprang out to display itself, naked and palpitating with unslaked desire. He now snaked his hand under her short skirt and rubbed her mound against the palm of his hand. A gentle moan of pleasure escaped from her throat as she lay back on the bean bag and Ivor found the waistband of her tights and pulled them over her hips and down to her ankles.

Carefully he unrolled the expensive sheer tights over her feet and by the time he reached to her groin, Sheena had unhooked her bra and skirt and lay naked except for her frilly white knickers above which he could see tufts of fluffy blonde muff he had previously seen only in her secret photographs. With trembling hands he now removed the panties and Sheena spread her legs invitingly, affording Ivor a bird's eye view of her glorious golden-haired pussey. His hands stroked her bare thighs and he moved higher to stroke the moist pussy lips that peeked through the fleecy blonde thatch, growling with delight as he continued to rub his fingers against her yielding slit.

She leaned forward and dragged him upwards, positioning his head between her legs and he buried his face in the wet hair that lightly covered her cunt. His heartbeat quickened and his prick bulged and throbbed against the rough material of the bean bag as his tongue raked along the length of Sheena's crack and then slipped down to probe inside. Almost of their own volition her legs splayed even wider as she sought to open herself further. Ivor slurped lustily as he drew her pouting pussy lips into his mouth, lapping up the pungent liquid which was flowing freely from her cunny. Her hips drew up in urgency as he frantically attacked her erect clitty which trembled and twitched at his electric touch. She clutched at his head and screamed with joy as he brought her off, flicking his tongue at a great speed in and out of her cunt as she orgasmed, her hips bucking as a flood of love juice came tumbling out of her cunny, soaking his face.

Sheena's soft body now relaxed as the tension snapped but the sight of Ivor's stiff, veined penis as he clambered up on top of her soon fired the quivering girl. She took hold of his thick prick and pulled it towards her until it wriggled its way into the crevice between her breasts. She then bent her head forward and pursed her lips tightly around his bared helmet, licking and sucking the tender cockflesh. Ivor eased back, taking his rigid rod from her mouth and wriggling down towards her blonde bush until his knob was poised at the entrance to her honeypot. He tenderly pushed forward and his delighted cock tingled exquisitely as it was enveloped by her clinging cunny. He sank down slowly until their pubic hairs matted together.

They bounced up and down on the bean bag. His cock throbbed violently as it slicked through her sopping cunt, in and out, and Ivor pulled her cunny lips open to ease the passage of his glistening wet cock. He tried to keep his strokes reasonably paced at first but the erotic sight of Sheena's ripe breasts and the contracting of her cunny muscles as he slewed his tool forwards and backwards excited him so much that almost immediately he began to fuck the beautiful, willing girl faster and faster with all the energy he could muster. His balls smacked against her raised bum and he felt an awesome climax building up. His cock, throbbing and as hard as a drill, made one final, frenzied lunge inside her juicy wetness before he exploded into her, jetting a tremendous spout of spunk which splattered against the walls of her cunny, sending erotic ripples of bliss throughout her body as she milked dry his twitching tool.

Yet Ivor sensed that she had not yet fully climaxed even as, with a smile, he rolled off her quivering body. He continued to pleasure her pussy, inserting one, two and finally three fingers inside her dripping cunt. She began to whimper uncontrollably as he found her clitty and he finger fucked her rhythmically, using the ball of his thumb to massage her erect little clitty. Her hips jerked wildly as she came in a sudden release. She clamped her thighs around his hand as she hugged him with gratitude for his consideration.

Ivor would have loved to stay and fuck the delicious girl for the rest of the afternoon and throughout the evening but, after they had recovered their senses, Sheena insisted that he leave before her flatmate Debbie returned from her visit to her family. 'Debbie's a very pretty girl and you'll probably want to try your luck with her, you randy so-and-so, but as her boy friend is the London middleweight judo champion I'm doing you a favour by not letting you meet her.'

'Ah, perhaps I had better leave then,' smiled Ivor as he pulled on his pants. 'I can't stand the sight of blood – especially my own! Seriously though, I hope that after today we'll be able to see more of each other.'

'I don't think there's any more of me left to see!' said Sheena, blowing him a kiss as she struggled into her tights.

'Oh come on, you know what I mean,' said Ivor as he buttoned up his shirt. 'I don't want you to feel this was just a one-off–'

She placed a finger on his lip and said gently. 'Let's play it by ear, Ivor. Don't make any rash promises because we've just made love. You have my 'phone number so give me a call when you get back from Scotland.'

'How did you know I was going to Scotland?' he asked in astonishment.

'Juliette told me on Thursday when I called to set up a meeting with you about publicising Sara Smith, Bob Maxwell's latest young discovery. We've scheduled a conference next Friday morning so I'll speak to you then if not before.'

'Okay, Sheena, I'll be in touch,' he said as he brought his car keys out of his pocket. 'Take care of yourself.' He kissed her good-bye and he set off back to his flat. As he drove back up Haverstock Hill to his own flat in West Hampstead, Ivor reflected how his love life always seemed to roller coaster through peaks and troughs. After a miserable month for them both, he had broken up with Caroline, his live-in girl friend, and was feeling very low when the invitation arrived for Billy Bucknall's no-holds-barred party at the Hunkiedorie. Now he had not only fulfilled an ambition by fucking the lovely Sheena but he also had the beautiful Samantha to call next month. There were other opportunities too to meet some new girls, not least the trip to Scotland which Sheena had mentioned. So with a little luck, Ivor concluded, his diary would be pretty hectic for the next few weeks!

A quiet Sunday evening in front of the television was on the agenda, he said to himself as he parked his car. Jimmy Bacon, another teenager from Bob Maxwell's stable of pop stars, was making his debut on *Sunday Night At The London Palladium*. It would earn him some brownie points if he called the impressario in the morning and congratulated him, for a spot on the peak-time TV show would sell thousands of Jimmy Bacon's new record and earn Maxwell – if not the young singer who had signed a fearsomely intricate contract – a great deal of money.

He swung his car into the forecourt of Barnicoat Mansions and parked his car. 'Hi there, Ivor, what brings you to this neck of the woods?' chirped a pert female voice directly behind him. 'You're a bit late for the party, almost everyone's gone except for Yvonne and Georgina and they'll be in bed with Julian by now.'

Ivor looked round to see a slim, dark-haired girl grinning at him. He remembered in an instant that she was a window dresser for one of the large West End department stores who coincidentally was a friend of Sheena's and who had been introduced by her to him when she would occasionally meet his secretary for lunch. 'Hello there,' he said with a warm smile, desperately trying to remember her name. 'I live in this block, actually, but whoever my neighbour is, I'm afraid he didn't invite me to his party.'

'What a shame, you missed a great thrash. Julian's just moved in and this was his flat-warming party. I must introduce you two as he's a Liverpudlian and doesn't know many people in London.'

'Well, he knows Yvonne and Georgina and they'll surely keep loneliness at bay for the time being.' Ivor mentally mouthed a prayer of thanks as his brain flashed the name of this attractive girl to his mouth. 'Who is this guy, Alison?'

She swept her hand through her dark curls. 'His name's Julian Saunders and he was the teens and twenties fashion buyer for our Northern stores. He's done so well that they've brought him to London to see if he can rejuvenate our ladies' wear sales. Our old chief buyer was a real idiot, always six months or more behind the times. But Julian doesn't just follow the herd, he's innovative and he'll push up sales.'

Her full lips curled with relish as with a gleam in her eyes she added: 'Mind, he's doing a different kind of pushing right now, isn't he? I must say that I envy Yvonne and Georgie, because the girls in Julian's office say he has a massive prick.'

'Lucky man,' said Ivor politely. 'So the party's over and he's tucked up in bed with two dolly birds.'

'Yes, and I'm stuck here waiting for a mini-cab which doesn't seem to be arriving,' said Alison grumpily. 'Honestly, these mini-cabs are so bloody unreliable, but I live in Willesden Green and to go home by public transport, especially on a Sunday, would take forever. Ivor, could I use your phone and ring the proper taxi people. It'll be more expensive but at least the black cabs are reliable and the drivers know where they're going. I don't want to go back to Julian's pad whilst he's having a bit of nookie. It wouldn't be appreciated and I don't want a black mark against my name in the office!'

'Of course you can phone for a cab from my flat. Come on up,' said Ivor hospitably. 'Just don't look too hard at all the mess. The porter's wife usually comes round on Tuesdays and Fridays but she's gone down with a chill and didn't come in last week.'

'Poor Ivor, had to do all your own cooking and cleaning, then?' she teased as they rode up in the lift to the second floor. 'I thought you had a live-in lady who took care of all that sort of thing.'

'I did until recently,' said Ivor as they stepped out of the elevator, 'but Caroline wasn't a Barbie doll kind of girl. She used to say that useless men were made not born and we shared all the chores. Still, thank goodness for Mrs Dawson, I just hope she'll be in on Tuesday. I've a washing machine, so that's no problem but there's a pile of ironing from the floor to the ceiling.'

'Have you got a shirt to wear for work tomorrow?' demanded Alison as Ivor opened the door of his flat. 'If you plug in the iron I'll do it for you with pleasure.'

In fact Ivor had bought a new shirt on Saturday morning for that very purpose. He had hung it up straightaway in his wardrobe so that some of the creases would disappear by Monday morning, but Alison's offer was too good to turn down.

So Ivor said: 'That's very kind of you, I'd be more than grateful. Look, I've also had an idea. Why don't you stay for a bite of supper and I'll run you home later.'

'Would you, Ivor? Well, thank you, that's a jolly good trade-off. Supper and a lift just for ironing a shirt! You must let me do at least two so you'll have one on Tuesday as well.'

'Okay, two shirts it is. Now, more important, how about a glass of white wine whilst I prepare supper. I can offer you omelettes with a side salad. How does that sound?'

Alison smiled and revealed two adorable dimples on her cheeks. 'Super, Ivor, I'd love an omelette. Only pour me a small glass of wine though please, there was masses to drink at Julian's party and I'm already feeling a little tired and emotional.'

By the time Alison had finished ironing the shirts Ivor had laid two places on his circular rosewood dining table. As she came into the room after washing her hands he struck a match and lit the rather naughty candle Martin Reece had given him on his return from a summer holiday in Thailand. Alison noticed at once that the pink candle was shaped like a squat, erect penis with two balls of wax completing the effect.

As they ate their omelettes Alison commented: 'You don't see candles like that in Woolworths.' Ivor explained that it was a gift from the Far East from his boss.

'Oh yes, well from what I've heard about you from

Sheena, Ivor Belling, a candle shaped little pussy would be more appropriate for your dining room!' Ivor smiled as he poured out some more wine.

'Oh, don't you believe everything Sheena told you about me.' But Alison looked steadily at him and replied: 'Now don't tell me that I'm going to be disappointed. We all have sexy secrets and one of mine has been about you since we met at your office. You were wearing a tight blue suit and though I'm not an inveterate crotch watcher I was turned on by the way your balls bulged through yor trousers. Don't look so shocked, girls have erotic fantasies just the same as boys do!'

She swallowed the rest of her wine and with a gleam in her eye she continued: 'It's been so frustrating lately – my boy friend's been sent to Wales for three weeks to work in our Cardiff store and to make matters worse, Victoria, the girl who shares a bedroom with me, has a new boy friend, Stan, who's been screwing the night away with her at least three times a week. He's a hunky young detective sergeant from the local nick who she met when the flat opposite was broken into last month. Stan's a bit thick, if you ask me but he's got a lovely big cock which he seems to keep stiff for hours at a time. So Vicki's enjoying herself whilst I have to lie under the sheets with my fingers in my ears. Mind you, the other night I decided to look across and I saw her giving him a really slurpy blow job. I felt myself getting very wet when he let fly as she gobbled his cock. He spunked so much that she couldn't swallow it all and the jism dripped down all over her tits.'

'Sounds like a very exciting evening,' drawled Ivor though this sexy story was making his prick stiffen perceptively in his trousers. 'On the other hand, I can sympathise with Vicki. I mean, it takes a lot of courage to be fucked in front of your room-mate. It's ever so difficult to relax even though I'm sure you didn't interrupt by laughing or making any sarcastic remarks.'

Alison giggled and said: 'I was very tempted to join in, especially when Vicki said it was her time of the month so

59

he would have to make do with being sucked off and wanked that night. But although I was feeling horny after watching Vicki suck on Stan's gleaming, thick cock, I just turned over and with great difficulty, simply closed my eyes and went to sleep.'

'How frustrating after being turned on like that,' sighed Ivor as he refilled her glass.

'Oh, watching doesn't turn me on so much,' said Alison with a glint in her eye. 'I prefer privacy and m'mm, this is nice wine, Ivor, much better than the plonk Julian was serving. I like to drink a little wine before lovemaking. It relaxes me like the nice soft lighting in your flat. I love screwing by candlelight – bodies look sexier in a dim glow.'

'Do you like music whilst making love?' asked Ivor, rising to stand behind her and placing his hands on her shoulders.

'Only sometimes,' she replied, reaching back to look up as their hands slipped together. 'Music sometimes distracts me and I like to concentrate on what I'm doing. If I hear a favourite song on the record player while I'm fucking my attention is drawn to the music. On the other hand, if the Rolling Stones are going full blast and I want to fuck badly enough, it simply doesn't matter.'

'How about the Beatles?' Ivor enquired softly as he released his hand to switch on his stereo.

'Well, the same applies – I only have to think of George Harrison and I go all weak at the knees.' She lifted her face up as Ivor bent down to kiss her. In a flash her mouth opened and her tongue was lashing around inside his mouth as he responded in kind.

Alison then rose up and they hugged each other tightly as their lips pressed together. Before very long they were on the sofa and Ivor was feeling the warmth of her ripe body through her silk blouse and thin skirt. His prick hardened to strain against the material of his trousers as he slipped open the buttons of her blouse. Thrilling to the discovery that Alison was wearing no bra, he stroked and moulded her magnificent firm breasts and tweaked the stiff nipples between his fingers. She sighed and groaned and ground her hips against him until Ivor worried that he was going to cream his new boxer shorts!

'It's more comfy in the bedroom,' he gasped and she silently nodded her head in agreement. They threw off their clothes before diving down together totally naked onto the soft mattress. Alison grabbed his pulsating prick, running her fingers along it, squeezing and rubbing the hot, velvet skin before teasing his uncapped helmet with her tongue. He thrust his slippery shaft deeper inside her mouth and she helped him by bobbing her head up and down, feeling his wiry pubic hair tickle her nose as she inhaled his perspiring fragrance.

She slurped noisily on his quivering cock but when she felt his body tremble and stiffen she lifted her mouth away and transferred her lips to his face as she muttered: 'Fuck me, Ivor, fuck me nice and hard with that big, throbbing prick, you randy lad.'

Ivor moved quickly, sliding himself on top of the lovely girl, pulling apart her juicy cunny lips which glistened with anticipatory lust. He slid himself on top of her as they moved, thighs together, until their pubic muffs rubbed roughly against each other. She grasped his cock and guided his knob between her pouting pussy lips. She wrapped her arms and legs around Ivor's lean, muscular frame and urged him on, clamping her feet round his back as he glided his yearning prick inside her soaking cunt. He pulled out and re-entered her juicy cunt again and again, thrusting as deeply as he could into her clinging crack. Her slick love channel clasped his shaft with each long, slow stroke and Ivor stayed still for a few moments, savouring to the full the delicious contractions of her cunt as it welcomed his cock into its portals.

They started to move together and Ivor treated the trembling girl to a slow, lazy fuck as he glided his shaft in and out of her tingling quim, sliding deeper and deeper inside her nookie with every thrust. Then he raised the tempo and their lips meshed together. Alison raised her buttocks as he plunged his prick into her willing pussy and her hips arched towards him as if trying to entice every inch of cock as far as possible inside her. Alison closed her eyes to enjoy the electric shocks of arousal that were rippling throughout every fibre of her being as Ivor's cock continued to pound away. Her sopping cunny clutched at his embedded penis as, with an anguished gurgle, they entered the last lap in the race. Their movements quickened and Ivor's cock drove in and out of her cunt faster and faster until, with a growl, he shot spasm after spasm of sticky white wodges of frothy sperm inside her. She shuddered into an explosive climax, her saturated cunt sending delicious waves of exquisite pleasure all over her quivering body.

Ivor rolled off the panting girl and lay on his back, gasping for air as he puffed: 'Wow! I'm sorry I came so soon but you're such a sexy lady that I couldn't hold back.'

'Don't worry, I came just after you spunked,' she replied, wiping a bead of perspiration from her brow. 'It was especially good for me because I haven't been fucked for a fortnight since I broke up with my boy friend.'

'What a waste, what a waste,' murmured Ivor, letting his fingers stray through her dark, damp cunny hairs until his palm pressed against her pussy.

Alison shrugged her shoulders. 'It was a mutual decision to end the relationship,' she said, pressing Ivor's hand firmly on her pubic mound. 'Ooh, that's nice, play with my pussy, I like that.

'No, it was time for Jeff and I to split up. He's a senior researcher for Rediffusion TV and when he had to go up to Scotland for a week a couple of months ago, I took off some holiday time to go with him. But I couldn't leave work till a couple of days after Jeff went up to Stirling and when I finally arrived at the hotel I was rather put out to discover that he had a young research assistant working with him, a pretty young teenage girl named Chrissie, and whilst of course we all had our own separate rooms, I had my suspicions that Jeff had already been fooling around with her by the time I signed the hotel register on the Tuesday afternoon.'

'What made you think so?' asked Ivor with interest.

'Well, it didn't need Sherlock Holmes to find out the score – as soon as I'd unpacked I thought I would go to Jeff's room and let him know I'd arrived, but just as I was about to knock on his door I heard a girl's voice say: "Honestly, Jeff, I've always preferred small cocks because they get so much harder and they're easier to manoeuvre inside my cunt. And honestly, it's only a small minority of guys who can boast more than six and half inches so your dimensions are pretty much the average. Anyhow, it's not what you do, it's the way that you do it which is all-important!"

'I gave two sharp raps on the door and called out "Jeff, it's me," and I heard some furtive scuffling which made me think at best they had been necking or that Jeff had been screwing her. "Just coming," he shouted out and I thought: "I'll bet you have!" Sure enough, when he answered the door his face looked flushed and I noticed his prick was bulging out of the front of his trousers. I went in and saw Chrissie (who I'd met before at the studios) smoothing down her skirt and slipping her feet into her shoes. I didn't say anything but inside I was seething as I was sure that I'd interrupted some heavy petting. Chrissie looked embarrassed and muttered some excuse about having some work to do, so she left Jeff and me alone. Of course at first he denied anything had happened but later confessed he had been finger-fucking the sexy little redhead under her skirt and she'd had is cock out and had been wanking him when I'd spoilt the party.

'It was hardly the best start to a holiday. I threatened to pack my bags and leave there and then though, in fact, I had no intention of leaving Jeff and Chrissie alone for a further week's paid-for fucking! So I let myself be mollified. Chrissie tactfully made an excuse about joining us for dinner and we had God knows how much wine with the meal. We staggered up to my room and I was so pissed that I just lay back and let Jeff undress me until I was completely naked. Then he took off his clothes and straddled himself over me, fondling his stiff cock up until the tip was touching my lips. I opened my mouth and started to suck him off, nibbling his knob the way I knew he loved best of all when out of the blue he said: "Alison, there's something about Chrissie that I think you ought to know." My mouth was filled with cock so I couldn't say anything but I just looked up to him as he continued: "She's awfully attractive don't you think? But believe it or not, she's bi-sexual and she fancies you more than me! How about letting her join us a little later on?"

'Looking back on it, all I can say is that Jeff was lucky that I was so far gone from all the booze he'd been pouring down my throat because though I was feeling incredibly randy, I might have been very angry at the very idea and I could have chomped my teeth down hard on his cock! But I'm ashamed to say that all I did was nod my head and Jeff said happily: "Great, I knew you'd be a great sport. I took the liberty of telling Chrissie I was sure it would be okay for her to come round in five minutes. I've left the door on the latch so we can finish what we've started."

'Well sure enough, a couple of minutes later in she walks as bold as brass. She shuts the door and immediately began undressing down to her black silk panties. As she walked across the room I couldn't help being turned on myself by her stunning looks. She was only just eighteen, fresh faced, fair skinned with a mass of bright red hair which tumbled down her back and a sleek trim body with small, jutting breasts and a flat belly. I couldn't help feeling a pang of jealousy at the way Jeff ogled her as she walked across the room nude except for her knickers. My resentment almost bubbled over when she climbed on the bed, sat on her haunches and began snogging with Jeff whilst I was still sucking his throbbing prick!

' "Pull her panties off, Alison," croaked Jeff and at this point I knew I had to obey him or simply walk out in a huff. Sorry, Ivor, but there's no prize for guessing what I did! I pulled the girl down on her back as I let Jeff's cock spring out of my mouth. He remained on his knees and started to lick and nip her large pink nipples whilst I wriggled down between her sleek thighs and yanked off her panties. Her springy pussy thatch was as red as the hair on her head and her long, inviting crack looked as if she could have taken Jeff's cock even if it had ten and half inches with ease! Her clitty popped out, the size of a small marble as I slipped my forefinger straight into her wet lovebox and I rubbed harder and harder until her clitty was as hard as a little rock. I slipped a second and third finger inside her juicy crack and spread the lips out wide which made her gurgle with pleasure. My lips were drawn irresistibly to her cunt and soon I was sucking away with all my might. Her delicious body writhed sensuously and Jeff continued to lap on her tits whilst I worked my tongue until my jaw ached, my tongue whipping wildly over her clitty until she was gushing so much that her pussy juices were streaming over my face.

'By now I wanted desperately to be fucked so I was delighted when Jeff rearranged us so that I was on my back and Chrissie was sitting astride my face with my tongue flicking dotingly around her cunt. He was just as keen to fuck me so he positioned himself behind Chrissie and cupped his hands under her firm young bum cheeks as his hard cock rammed its way inside my cunny. I gasped with pleasure as I felt him penetrate me to the hilt and as he built up his rhythm I could feel his ballsack swinging heavily against my arse.

'Soon I could feel the waves of a second orgasm surging out from my pussy. "Go on, Jeff, nice and quick now, I'm going to come! Push your cock in harder! Push it in, push, push, aaaah!" Closing my eyes and sucking greedily on Chrissie's sopping quim I thrust my hips upwards to meet Jeff's powerful pumping, driving him deeper and harder inside me. Then we both came together – I was first and not only was I threshing around like a scalded cat but my strong cunny muscles were contracting, squeezing and milking Jeff's thick prick. I wrapped my legs around his strong trunk so that his spurting cock was jammed inside my love channel.

'Almost instantly his hands squeezed my titties as his shaft throbbed as he sent a stream of warm, creamy spunk cascading into my waiting cunt. His cock quivered as he ejaculated again and again. I must say that not even you, Ivor, spend as much as Jeff. I've never fucked a man whose nuts produce so much jism as Jeff Parkinson's big balls, even though his cock is only of average size.

'My fervent tonguing now brought Chrissie off and she pushed off Jeff, who was absolutely exhausted after fucking me, and wriggled herself between my legs. She played with my pussy, drawing the lips apart and diddling my cunt with the tip of her finger. "What a delicious pussy you have, Alison, darling," she said almost matter-of-factly. "Such a lovely little round clitty and a wonderful deep red cunt. How it sucks in and presses my finger. Honestly, if only I had a prick I would love to fuck you with it." She kissed my sopping muff and I felt totally uninhibited as she stroked my quvering thighs. She had a marvellous light touch and I relaxed completely, bathing in this marvellous glow which flowed out from my pussy. I looked down and saw her fiery red hair bobbing up and down between my white thighs as I opened my legs and arched my body upwards to meet the thrusts of her darting tongue. Her hands moved up to tweak my erect nipples and rhythmically she began to lap inside my pussy lips whilst the hard ball of her thumb rubbed lewdly against my clitty. I screamed with excitement as sizzling crackles of ecstacy shot through my cunt and I exploded into yet aother thrilling climax whilst Chrissie continued relentlessly to lap up the liquid mixture of love juices and jism which was pouring out of my pussy.

'We sucked and fucked together throughout the night

and I was so tired that I stayed in bed whilst Chrissie and Jeff had breakfast. "We'll be at the Castle all morning if you would like to meet us there," said Jeff as they left for work. I mumbled that I would see them there about mid-day. Well, I've never really been one for lazing the day away especially as it was a gloriously sunny morning, and by half past ten I was already walking up the steep hill towards Stirling Castle. I had taken my camera as Jeff had told me that there were some splendid views from the battlements.'

Alison breathed deeply as she continued. 'How right he was, though some of the photographs were rather more suitable for *Ram* than anywhere else! For while I was resting in the lovely Queen Anne Garden I thought I heard a familiar noise coming from behind a secluded clump of bushes some fifty yards away. I took out my camera and zoomed in – and through the viewfinder I could see Jeff's bare bum bouncing up and down between a shapely pair of legs.'

'Good grief, he was fucking Chrissie yet again. My God, you have to give your old boy friend full marks for stamina, if nothing else,' remarked Ivor lazily, rubbing his fingers more insistently along the edges of her hairy crack.

'Maybe,' she said grimly. 'But in fact who should suddenly come by and quickly dive into the bushes but a pretty red-headed girl! So who was he screwing?'

'Bloody hell! What aftershave does Jeff use? Order me a dozen bottles immediately!' laughed Ivor but he fell silent when he saw Alison was not amused. Nevertheless, she managed a tiny, wry smile as she said: 'I was dumbfounded and so angry that I hurtled down to the garden and ran towards the bushes. Of course, I'd come to the same conclusion as you but in fact Jeff *was* fucking Chrissie. The girl who had joined them was actually Chrissie's cousin. She had her knickers down and was lying alongside Chrissie with her head underneath Jeff sucking his balls while Chrissie was finger fucking her pussy.

'I was so shocked that I said nothing but I took a few photographs before walking away. They were so engrossed in their fucking that they didn't even know that I'd seen them. Anyhow, I walked back to the hotel and packed my bags. What hurt more is that I didn't check out of the hotel till past one o'clock. Though I hadn't turned up at the Castle Jeff hadn't come back to see where I was or even telephoned to call and find out if I had left a message for him. So I didn't leave a good-bye note for him when I left the hotel.

'And that's about it, Ivor, I took the train to Glasgow and came back to London that afternoon. I haven't seen Jeff since although when he did telephone me that evening I simply told him that I couldn't handle his free and easy lifestyle. He had asked me to be faithful and naturally I had assumed that he wouldn't play around. So I feel he betrayed me – there's no point in having a relationship if you can't trust your partner. I suppose what hurt me most was his total lack of honesty. If Jeff had told me that he was fucking Chrissie and her cousin (and he admitted he had been screwing them both for at least four months) at least I would have known where I stood. As it was, I had been prepared to forgive his indiscretion and I'd even joined in his little romp. Sure, I'd enjoyed it – but I couldn't cope with yet more deceit. I don't think any man or woman would have stood for such behaviour.'

Ivor nodded and said: 'I can't disagree with you, Alison. Do unto others as you would be done by is the rule I've honestly tried to follow.' He kissed her pussy and her crisp dark hairs tickled his nostrils. 'Atchoo!' he sneezed and his inadvertent action immediately lightened the atmosphere.

'Ivor Belling, you are a very naughty boy,' she scolded lightly. 'It is very poor form to sneeze into a lady's cunt.'

'My sincere apologies,' grinned Ivor, kissing Alison's pussy lips with a noisy smack. 'Let me show you just how sorry I am.' And he sank two fingers into her sticky, damp cunt which was ready to be pleasured by his swelling organ. She miaowed with delight and wriggled over onto her belly, scrambling up on all fours and pushing out her ripe white buttocks. Ivor needed no second invitation to position himself behind her and slide his stiff member between her bum cheeks, plunging his throbbing tool all the way inside her. At first he stayed fairly still and he watched Alison's hips rotate in an erotic circular motion as she pressed her face and elbows into the pillow.

He reached round with his hand and nipped her erect clitty with his long fingers. This sent Alison into a frenzied ecstacy. 'Oooooh! That's glorious,' she yelled with abandon. 'More, more, pump your fat cock into me, Ivor! Ooooh! Aaaah! Ooooh! Yes, yes, yes!'

The bed rocked as Ivor clutched at her breasts with his other hand, rubbing her nipples until they stood up like little red stalks whilst he diddled her clitty and his excited stiff penis thrust in and out of her saturated slit. His natural preferred pace matched Alison's own favourite rhythm and he brought her off twice and then, with a final convulsive shudder, his cock spewed out luscious jets of creamy jism. They sank down together happily as his prick jerked wildly whilst her clinging cunny milked it dry.

They lay in silence until Alison noticed that Ivor had come so fully that much of his sticky ejaculation of spunk had dribbled down her legs along with the rivulets of her own juices and the formerly snowy white sheet now exhibited a large wet stain.

'Oh dear, we'll have to change the bedclothes,' said Alison but Ivor would have none of it. 'Don't worry, it'll dry,' he said. 'And in any case if it's still there on Tuesday we'll have given my charlady, Mrs Dawson, a cheap thrill.'

Later that evening Ivor drove his surprise but very welcome guest back to her flat in Willesden Green. 'Alison, how about doing this again next week?' murmured Ivor as he opened the car door for her.

She looked at him quizically and said: 'Do you mean it, Ivor, or are you just being polite? It's such a typically

English expression to say "we must get together one day" when you don't really mean such a thing!'

'I know what you mean but I do genuinely want to see you again,' protested Ivor as he walked up the front drive with her. She paused for a moment and then planted a little kiss on his cheek. 'I'd like to see you again too, Ivor, but it's all happened so quickly and unexpectedly for both of us,' she said, taking out a card from her handbag and passing it to him. 'Tell you what, phone me on Thursday evening after seven o'clock on this number. Is that okay?'

'I'll phone you on Thursday night,' Ivor promised and he returned Alison's kiss before walking back to his car. On the short journey home he reflected that though he had made love to three beautiful girls over the weekend, he and all the girls were unsure whether or not any lasting relationship would come about from their frenetic couplings.

Only time would tell, said Ivor to himself, as he yawned and set his mind on tomorrow's important meeting. He would have to do his level best to persuade Cable's potential new client to sign on the dotted line. By the time he had returned to Barnicoat Mansions Ivor was feeling very tired, though he remembered to set the alarm before he fell into bed. Within five minutes he was fast asleep.

THREE

Stiff As A Poker

It was easier for Ivor to catch the Underground train from West Hampstead than to drive into town and then spend the rest of the day fretting about feeding the parking meters. This Monday morning, as usual, he managed to find a seat in the carriage but Ivor always offered up his seat if he saw an older woman standing in the peak-time commuter crush.

Although he had slept well, he was still feeling a little tired from his bedroom exploits over the weekend. He deliberately buried his face in the *Guardian* when the train stopped at Finchley Road where the carriage invariably filled up to bursting point. He tried to read about the efforts of Prime Minister Harold Wilson to achieve a settlement with the rebel white settlers in Rhodesia, keeping his eyes firmly upon the columns of newsprint. But in the last resort he settled, as always, for principle. Looking over the top of his newspaper, he saw almost directly in front of him a small silver-haired lady clinging to a rail as the train rocked along the winding tunnel to Baker Street.

With a sigh he folded his paper and stood up. 'Would you like to sit down?' he said politely to the elderly lady. She smiled gratefully at him but, before she could move, a tall, gangly youth plumped himself down on Ivor's seat.

'Excuse me, but I got up to give this lady my seat,' said Ivor. The spotty young man ignored the remark and opened out his newspaper.

Ivor breathed heavily, tapped the intruder on the shoulder and tried again. 'Perhaps you didn't hear what I just said – I gave up this seat for the lady standing next to me.'

'Did you now? Well she can have it when I get out at Oxford Circus.'

In any other country someone else would surely come to his aid, he thought. But when Ivor glanced about him, every single one of the many male passengers, as if under orders, studiously avoided catching his eyes. As was normal in the morning rush-hours, the train slowed to a standstill in the tunnel just outside Baker Street station. The silence was broken only by the faint buzzing noise from the tubes of flourescent light. I must be bloody barmy, he muttered very softly. The youth's sneering, self-assured tone had riled Ivor, he had been badly bullied for a time at his secondary school until after his fourteenth birthday when he had suddenly shot up in height and weight and could take good care of himself.

'Look here, are you getting out of that seat or do I have to pull you out of it?' he said angrily, raising his voice to ensure that as many of the sheepish fools around them who were desperately wanting to avoid any involvement could hardly fail to hear the argument.

'Piss off, fuck-face,' sneered the youth insultingly. 'If I wanted to hear from an arsehole, I'd fart.'

'It doesn't matter, don't take no notice of him,' pleaded the woman who Ivor had stood up for in the first place.

'Yes it does,' he replied and he passed her his newspaper. 'Hold that for me, please. Then he drew back his fist and punched through the youth's newspaper, feeling his knuckles scrape on the rough surface of his adversary's eyebrows.

With a bellow the tall youngster stood up and produced a wicked-looking flick knife from the pocket of his jeans. 'I'll cut your balls off for that, you fucking shit,' he screamed but before he could attempt to carry out his threat a graceful blonde girl dug the point of her umbrella sharply in his groin. He yelled out in pain as he doubled over, clutching himself between the legs and Ivor smashed his fists downwards on the back of the neck to send him sprawling to the floor. The girl coolly kicked the knife further away from his hand as the train lurched forward into Baker Street Station.

'Someone call a porter and hand this ruffian over to the police,' suggested a portly man who, a moment before, had gazed earnestly at the advertisement for a ladies' hairdresser rather than even glance across to the altercation six feet away from his seat.

'I don't want to bother with the police, let's just chuck him off the train,' said Ivor briskly, grabbing the groaning would-be knifer's jacket and hauling him to his feet. 'We've all got to get to work and there's no point wasting time on scum like him.'

He hauled the youth to his feet and pushed him out onto the platform. 'You come within five yards of me next time and I'll break your arms,' he hissed as he stepped smartly back inside the carriage before the doors shut.

'Thank you very much for your help,' he said to the courageous blonde girl who had picked up the knife.

'My pleasure, I hate to see such horrible behaviour. There was no reason for him for behaving like a boor.' The old lady, now safely in her seat, lifted her head and said: 'I would like to thank you as well. What is the matter with young men like that? What on earth was he trying to prove?'

Now the incident was over the other passengers joined in the conversation and Ivor correctly surmised that among them were people who had travelled in the same carriages for the past five years and never before exchanged even a cursory greeting were now at least talking to each other. When the train reached Oxford Circus he was pleased to see that his extremely pretty ally also left the train but his hopes of further contact were dashed. She flashed a smile at him and waved goodbye as she made her way to the exit whilst he made his way towards the Central Line escalator.

Nevertheless, his eventful journey made for an interesting talking point when he arrived at the office. His new secretary, the svelte, dark Juliette Burillo was most impressed and said as she handed Ivor a mug of hot coffee: 'I just cannot understand how some men believe that women admire this *macho* attitude. Perhaps some silly teenage kids look up to boys who strut around like peacocks – but give me the old-fashioned gentle approach every time!

'Quite right, Juliette,' said Martin Reece cheerfully as he bustled into the room. 'I don't know what you're talking about but I'm sure that I agree with you!'

'Super! I was just saying that Cable should pay every secretary a summer bonus of two weeks' wages next month!'

'Why not?' said Martin heartily. 'If we land this new account I think all the secretaries should get something extra in their pay packets. Pity that I'm making you a junior account executive if Ivor can persuade Mark Hamilton to give us his publicity account.'

She looked puzzled as Martin continued: 'He's the managing director of Golden Tan Capsules which give the skin a bronzed look without sitting in the sun.' Juliette looked doubtful and Ivor said: 'Its true, you can tan without the sun, no more blistering or peeling.'

'You'll look healthier, more energetic and attractive with a tan,' intoned Martin, reading from the sheet of paper he was carrying in his hand. 'Your friends will be amazed and will compliment you whilst you'll turn heads everywhere with your golden bronzed skin.'

'And Golden Tan Capsules are 100% safe,' added Ivor, standing up and placing his hand on Martin's shoulders. 'Probably even more safe than the ultra violet radiation from the sun as there's no risk of any damage to your skin.'

Juliette tossed back her head and smoothed her hand sensuously along her rich, black locks of short hair.

'Sounds wonderful,' she said with a distinct lack of enthusiasm. 'But with my colouring I think I can afford to pass.'

'Maybe *you* can, you lucky girl,' conceded Ivor. 'Though Mark assures me that the little pills also darken natural tans. Anyhow, he'll be here in twenty minutes so the best of luck. Remember, I'm going to meet him, wheel him in here to talk with you and then make myself available for a final word before he leaves us. I'd have liked to have offered Mark lunch but he has a meeting with a big wholesaler early this afternoon.'

Although they both had some little reservation about his product, both Ivor and Juliette liked the cut of Mark Hamilton's jib when Martin introduced the entrepreneur to them. He was a handsome, broad built man of perhaps thirty-five. Craggy faced with well pronounced cheekbones, a firm mouth and a square jaw, his hair was turning prematurely grey. Ivor wondered whether Mark Hamilton had been taking his own tablets because his colour suggested that he had just come off the beach of the ultra-fashionable Spanish resort of Marbella.

'Nice to meet you, Ivor,' he said pleasantly. 'Martin Reece has said some very complimentary things about you.' Ivor in turn won favour with Juliette by introducing her as his personal assistant rather than as his secretary.

'Hi, there,' said Mark Hamilton with a cordial handshake. 'Nice to meet you too, Juliette, though I don't think there's any need to offer you any of our capsules.'

'Well I'm not sure if your tan comes out of a bottle,' she said. He shook his head with a grin and retorted: 'I'd be dishonest if I didn't tell you that I only came back from Miami three days ago. You see, now that the tablets have been given full approval by the United States Food and Drug Administration, we've appointed an American distibutor for Golden Tan Capsules. I went across to Florida to sign the deal – ironic really, because it's known as the Sunshine State. But the chap we've decided to deal

75

with, a man named Ted Mottram, is based there and he has a good team of reps calling on wholesale and retail druggists throughout the country.'

He refused the offer of coffee and Juliette took notes as he explained how his business was run. 'Rod Burbeck, a scientist friend of mine from London University, had the original idea for Golden Tan Capsules. When we decided to market the pills, he bought a third of the firm's shares and I put up the rest of the capital. It took a while for the word to get around but once we could assure everyone that they were perfectly safe, that's when it all started to happen for us. I quit my sales manager job with Horne Manufacturing, the shoe people in Northampton, to work full-time for our company and we've built up quite a good little business. At first we sold exclusively through mail-order – you might have seen our ads in the press with the pretty girl in the bikini with the line "At Last You Can Tan Without The Sun".'

'Where are the pills produced?' enquired Ivor.

'We started in my garden but now we're renting a small factory unit in Bletchley. The tablets are easy enough to manufacture and are absolutely harmless to man or beast. The main ingredient is beta carotene which is widely used as a food colouring. I don't know too much about what else goes into them but we've been given the green light by the Americans and they are far more tougher about these things than over here. Anyway, since we decided to sell the pills through chemists and supermarkets we've trebled our turnover, but we can't afford to spend vast sums on advertising. So I thought we would see if a public relations agency could help us. I've seen a couple of agencies already but so far I haven't been greatly impressed. Then an old colleague of mine in Horne's publicity division recommended me to Martin Reece and that's how I came to be here.'

Ivor tapped his pen on his notebook and asked: 'Well, you're obviously marketing a successful product. But what about the marketing problems? Sluggish demand? Competition? Price resistance? Lack of distribution?'

'Not much competition and I don't think price is too much of an obstacle. The course requires you to take two capsules daily for a fortnight and then two more daily. A jar of sixty capsules only costs three pounds and frankly that gives everyone a damned good gross profit margin. I'm sure the demand for the capsules is there because you only have to look at how successful we've been already, but we do need far more shops selling *and* displaying them for us. We now have two full-time reps and four agents covering the country for us, while I look after the big chains. We need all the help we can get to persuade the trade to stock our product.'

'Yes, it's obvious that you need a demand-led publicity campaign,' said Ivor thoughtfully. 'A plan which will get potential customers asking their chemist for Golden Tan Capsules and give you and your reps that extra bit of leverage to excite the buyer.'

Mark Hamilton sighed and said: 'You've hit the nail on the head, but our problem is that the company can't afford too much at present. We can't exist just on one line and Rod Burbeck, my partner, is developing a new slimming product which means that most of our profits are being ploughed straight back in the business.'

There was silence for a moment or two and then Ivor snapped his fingers and said: 'Look, there are some issues which I think we must study in depth. Packaging, for example, and then you need to ask whether you should sell only through the pharmacy trade. Market research can help you find out who buys the capsules – though I suspect that women make up eighty per cent of your market. But we do need to get cracking straightaway to hit the market just before the summer.

'Why don't you feature a lovely girl in the ads you are running – what we could do is build up a story about her. You know we do a lot of work for Bob Maxwell, the pop promoter – we could get pictures of the girl with Ruff Trayde or Jimmy Bacon into the papers and of course she'll always have this lovely golden skin colour which she'll tell everyone comes from your capsules.'

'If we use a blonde girl, we could say that she can't sit in the sun because she burns easily,' said Juliette excitedly. 'But she always looks so wonderful because she takes Golden Tan Capsules.'

Ivor nodded his approval. 'At the beginning we probably won't get a complete plug but it's the idea of tanning without the sun we need to get across. As you're the market leader that'll help you far more than any competitor.'

Mark Hamilton's craggy face broke into a broad grin. 'I like the idea – but do you think you can pull it off?'

'Sure,' said Ivor confidently. 'The popular papers love the chance to run a photograph of a pretty girl and we'll provide them with an excuse.'

Half an hour later Martin Reece popped his head through the door and shortly afterwards Cable Publicity's newest client had signed a contract. 'I'm sorry you haven't time to stay for lunch,' said Martin and Mark Hamilton consulted his watch. 'Well, I suppose I've got time for a quick bite,' he said and so Ivor asked Juliette to telephone Yummies and order smoked salmon sandwiches for three.

Martin opened a bottle of white wine and the three men enjoyed a relaxed lunch. Ivor asked Mark Hamilton how he had enjoyed his trip to Florida. 'It was marvellous,' he replied enthusiastically. 'Between ourselves though, the first day was best of all.

'I arrived the day before I was due to see anyone on business as I wanted to be fresh and on the ball for some important meetings. So I spent the afternoon on the hotel beach and not surprisingly I fell asleep in my chair. A hand patted my face and I woke up to see a stunning blonde girl in a bikini bending over me. "I hope you don't mind, but I thought I'd wake you as you might get sun burned if you stay out here much longer," she said in a friendly drawl. "Thanks very much, that's really kind of you," I replied and we struck up a conversation. She guessed I was English from my accent and she told me how much she'd enjoyed a vacation in London two years ago. We went into the sea for a swim and afterwards she asked me to put some sun-tan lotion on her back as she lay face down on a towel and undid the strap of her bikini. I dabbed some cream on her glowing skin and just looking at her lithe young body made my prick bulge in the tight front of my swimming costume. She looked up directly between my legs and passed her tongue over her top lip.

'"Why don't you go and wash away all the sand and salt water in the showers?" she suggested and I readily agreed if for no other reason than to hide my embarrassment at the swelling mound between my legs. She told me that her name was Judy, by the way, and that she was an entertainments hostess at the hotel. I waved goodbye to her and headed for a much-needed cool shower. The shower room was quite simple, a few overhead pipes and shower heads over a wet sand floor. Thin streams of sunlight filtered through the crisscrossed slats of the thin wooden wall. There was no lock on the door so though I was alone, my eyes closed and savouring the cold jet of water flowing down on my heated body. Then I heard the door creak open.

'I felt a soft pair of hands flutter over my shoulders. "Would you like me to soap you down?" I heard Judy's voice ask me. I opened my eyes and turned my head out of the cascading water jet to look at her. Oh boy, did she look sexy! Her large breasts were overflowing out of her tiny bikini which barely covered her nipples and the shower spray glistened in the inviting cleft between her jiggling breasts. The bottom of her bikini was little more than a G-string and the glimpses of pale skin just beyond her tan lines made my prick stir again.

'"That would be wonderful," I said to her and slowly, sensually she soaped my chest and kneaded my thighs and

79

calves as she dropped to her knees, bringing her face level to my rising cock. Then without a word she rolled down the elastic waistband of my costume over my stiff shaft and pulled my trunks down to the ground. I stepped out of them and turned the shower down to a trickle as Judy took a handful of soapy cream and lathered me all over from my balls to the tip of my cock. She rinsed me clean and bathed me again but this time with her slithering tongue. She lapped all round my knob which drove me so wild I thought I'd shoot off there and then but then as she started licking my balls I suddenly thought, *My God! Someone could easily walk in on us!*

'Yet strangely enough the tension was an extra turn-on and I was just about to spunk inside Judy's mouth when she pulled away and stood up. "I could also use some cooling down, Mark. My turn now, huh?" she said huskily as she ripped off her bikini top and exposed the biggest pair of juicy erect red nipples I think I've ever seen. Then she wriggled down the bottom half and I caught my breath when I saw her dark, thick thatch of pubic hair which was already wet by both the shower and her own juices.

'I took another deep breath and, starting at her slender neck, I soaped her back and worked my way around to her front, massaging her breasts with my slippery fingers. Her eyes were half closed, her hips swaying as if in a hypnotic trance. I cupped my hand over her gorgeous black bush, rubbing the protruding little clitty with my middle finger. But Judy immediately pushed my hand aside and pressed herself into my throbbing stiffie, drawing my shaft about two or three inches inside her which was just enough to drive her crazy. Arching her back, she raised herself on tiptoe, forcing my tool deeper inside her as I held her by the hips and thrust back, my cock pumping in and out of her squelchy cunt.

'"I want you in me all the way!" she moaned as my cock slipped out of her pussy and slid upwards against her tummy. She took hold of my prick and pulled me across to a bench on which we had both thrown our towels.

'We now put it to much better use! Judy turned her back to me and bent over the bench. I grabbed the deliciously quivering cheeks of her tight little arse and pulled them apart, my cock sliding into the crevice between them as I entered her squishy honeypot from behind. She pushed her hips back at me, plunging me all the way inside her cunt. She pressed her face and elbows into the towels and raised her bum and from this angle, I could see my knob sliding in and out of her sopping love channel. On the downstroke, her cunny lips distended; then they contracted as she drew me back in.

'Holding on to those gorgeous bum cheeks I pounded in and out of her with long, deep strokes. She squealed with delight as my balls slapped against her bottom. With a shudder I felt her come and then I let go, drenching her cunt with fierce shoots of hot spunk. We both wanted to continue for we were having too good a time to let it end there, so we slipped on our costumes and spent the rest of the evening in the privacy and comfort of my suite.'

'Very nice, very, very nice,' commented Martin Reece with a glint in his eyes. 'Mark, we must take you to the Hunkiedorie, a discreet little club we go to occasionally when we've something to celebrate.'

'Meanwhile, Ivor has a nice job to do – choosing a girl for the Golden Tan promotion,' grinned Mark Hamilton. Later that afternoon, after his client had left for his appointment at a drug wholesaler, Ivor rang Leon Standlake at the Churchmill Agency and explained the situation to him. 'Leave it to me, Ivor. When can I send some girls round to see you? I've some lovely new girls on the books,' said the bustling Mr Standlake whose model agency specialised in providing glamorous pin-ups for newspapers and magazines throughout Europe.

'I'm in all day tomorrow, Leon,' answered Ivor. 'Usual terms and I really need a cracker. Don't waste your girls' time or mine by sending round anyone except the very best of the bunch.'

'Point taken,' agreed the agent. 'But while they're

there, what about Ronnie Bloom's new swimsuits catalogue? You used Elaine and Angela last time and I presume you want two new girls this year.'

'You're right, we'll need two girls for a shoot in a couple of months. Okay, we might as well kill two birds with one stone. I'll need a blonde and a brunette, both size tens for Ronnie Bloom and a light skinned blonde girl for this new account.' He put down the telephone and leaned back in his chair with a smirk of satisfaction – choosing a sexy model for a promotion was one of his favourite jobs.

In the meantime he had a report to write for an important client. He drifted across the room to Juliette's office but his secretary was not at her desk. He pulled the Bresslaw Industries folder from out of the filing cabinet but to his astonishment, as he was leaving, he noticed a copy of *Ram* magazine half-hidden beneath some papers on Juliette's desk. What on earth was she doing with a raunchy men's magazine? He wondered whether Sheena had told Juliette about her involvement with Brian Lipman and his model Janice but then he remembered Sheena telling him that the sexy photographs wouldn't appear in the magazine until later in the year.

Ivor pushed the papers away and looked at the magazine, which was open at the letters page. One letter had been ringed in a black circle by Juliette and Ivor picked up the magazine and quietly read the letter out loud.

'Dear Editor, I am twenty years old and work in a publicity agency in London. I work for a hunky looking man of about thirty who I know fancies me but he seems to be very shy and I think I will have to take the first step if I'm ever going to get him to fuck me.

'I know he is a keen tennis player and my fantasy is that one day after work we'll play tennis at his club and after a few games I'll pretend to hurt my ankle. Then, when he comes to see what's wrong, I'll hold his arm and let him help me to the changing room. Then, whilst he is putting away our gear, I'll lock the door and sidle up to him. "My

*foot's much better now, Ivor," I'll say and then as if he
could read my mind he'll cover my face with his lips and
we'll kiss. Then he'll put his hands under my shirt and
unclasp my brassiere before pulling open the buttons at the
front of my shirt and cupping my breasts with his hands.
We'll sink to the floor as he kisses all round my big red
nipples and then sucks in one into his mouth while he feels
under my skirt with one hand to pet my wet pussy whilst he
tears open the buttons of his shorts with the other. I let my
hand stray across to his groin and my palm rubs against his
huge erection as he wriggles out of his shorts and underpants. A thrill rushes through me as I grasp his naked cock,
hot and hard against my fingers as I squeeze it and it
pulsates with his forefinger on my throbbing clitoris. I gasp
as he moves his finger all along my saturated crack and lie
back for him to slide his delicious big cock in my slippery
slit.*

'*At last the time has come and I spread my legs and arch
my back as he steers the knob of his lovely cock between the
lips of my raging love-box and he comes into me carefully,
wrapping his arms around me and burying his face in my
hair. Then he rams his thick length home, steering his knob
deep inside my sopping hole as he penetrates me fully,
massaging every fibre of my cunt, sending me into
deliriums of pure joy. He whispers: "You're so beautiful,
Juliette, so incredibably lovely," and this makes me come
with pulsing stabs of pleasure and then he fills my cunny
with his hot sperm which sends me into a world of total
ecstacy . . .*

'*But though writing this uncensored wishful thinking is
making my panties wet, what can I do to turn fantasy into
reality?*'

J.B.
London S.W.6

'Good God, Juliette wants me to fuck her,' breathed
Ivor whose prick was naturally hard as rock and straining
for release from the confines of his trousers. 'Bloody hell,
she didn't have to write to *Ram*, all she had to do was ask!'

83

Ivor swung round with the magazine in his hand as the door clicked open and Juliette came in the room with an armful of folders to be filed. She took one look at Ivor and dumped the files heavily on her desk. 'Oh no, don't tell me that you've read that fucking letter!' she groaned. 'Well yes, I have, Ivor admitted. 'Why on earth didn't you tell me Juliette, why I'm honoured, I really am, look, are you doing anything tonight, I –'

She interrupted him with a sweeping movement of her hands. 'Ivor, I'm sorry but I didn't write the letter in that dreadful magazine.'

His mouth sagged open and he gaped at the vivacious, dark haired beauty. 'You didn't write it? But the initials are yours, you live in S.W.6 and you work for a publicity agency.'

'I know, I know,' she groaned, 'and I'll murder my girl friend, Naomi. She's a medical student and desperately strapped for cash and she wrote that letter to *Ram*, not me. Look at the top of the letters page – they pay ten guineas for each printed and fifteen for the star letter of the month.'

Ivor looked hard at the page and then roared with laughter. 'Well, at least she copped the star prize – but she's a very naughty girl to use my name and your initials.'

'Yes, I gave her a good telling-off when I saw the letter yesterday. I mean, she did tell me she was going to try her luck but I never knew . . .' her voice trailed off and she suddenly grinned. 'If it makes you feel any better, Ivor, Naomi does rather fancy you. Don't you remember seeing her in reception on Thursday after work? She came to the office as I took her to Bob Jackson's party in Kentish Town. We had supper first with Claire Trewin from accounts and changed at her flat rather than go home all the way to Chelsea and then have to trek all the way back to North London.'

'Of course I remember her and I'm very flattered,' said Ivor with evident sincerity. He was indeed more happy to have heard that his praises had been sung in this way by

Juliette's attractive friend. 'She's rather petite, with a full figure and lovely big dark eyes.

'Which are nice but not so nice as yours, of course!' he said hastily and Juliette giggled. 'It's alright, Ivor, I don't mind. Naomi *is* very pretty and she does have lovely big eyes.

'She's got big bosoms too if you want to know, much bigger than mine,' she added wickedly, flashing a quick glance at Ivor's crotch which was still looking well-filled, 'but I don't suppose you'd be interested in taking her out, would you?'

'Who says?' said Ivor indignantly. 'I'd love to meet her again. We did speak for a couple of minutes whilst you were in the loo and I thought she was a smashing girl.'

Juliette looked mischievously at him. 'Well, if you really mean it, I wish you'd try your luck this evening. Naomi and I are meeting for a drink after work and then I'd like to slip off by six o'clock. Bob Jackson's asked me out to dinner and I won't feel guilty about leaving Naomi if I know that you'll be taking her somewhere nice.'

So she's going to go out with Bob Jackson, mused Ivor who was somewhat surprised to hear the news. Bob was a handsome young lad from Leeds whom Martin had taken on about six months ago to service a group of motor car showrooms which had unexpectedly engaged Cable Publicity from a short list of four agencies after Martin had taken the sales director to an evening at the Hunkie-dorie Club. Bob had swiftly earned himself quite a reputation as a well-hung stud amongst the girls in the office. Only the other day he had overheard two of the girls giggling over the rumoured measurements of Bob Jackson's organ which, apparently, had been seen during his recent wild party which Juliette and Naomi had attended. 'Liz said it was like a third arm,' Adele from the post room had declared. Ivor idly wondered what Juliette would find out the actual truth about the proportions of the young Yorkshireman's prick.

'I'd be delighted to take her out,' said Ivor. 'Does she

like Chinese food? I was going to get a take-away and have a quiet evening in but I'll gladly book a table at the Yangtse in Gerrard Street instead.'

'Marvellous, Naomi loves Chinese food so you've something in common already!'

'Well, can you ring her this afternoon and see how she feels about it? She might not be as keen on me as you think.'

'Bet with folding money and I'll give you odds of a hundred to one,' said Juliette. Her confidence was borne out during a hasty and excited telephone call. 'There we are, everything's arranged. Naomi will come here directly from her last lecture. She's at the Middlesex Hospital so it's only a ten minute walk away.'

They managed to clear a sizeable amount of paperwork from Ivor's desk that afternoon and both were more than ready to call it a day when spot on five forty five a call came through that Naomi was waiting in reception. 'Come on, Juliette, let's leave on time for a change,' said Ivor, who was looking forward eagerly to seeing Naomi again. She was even more attractive than he had remembered, with a mop of dark hair and a pretty face with large, expressive eyes and a full figure. Juliette's light-hearted comment about Naomi's big breasts was right eough, thought Ivor as she brushed past him as he held the door open on the way into the saloon bar of the *The Cat and Compass*.

Ivor bought three large gin and tonics and they settled themselves down in a comfortable corner of the bar. 'Did you always want to be a doctor, Naomi?' he asked. 'It's a real calling, isn't it, not like being professional layabouts like Juliette and myself. Did you have a nurse's uniform when you were a little girl?'

She smiled and revealed two rows of sparkling white teeth. 'Sure, and I loved to wear it whilst I bandaged all my dollies. Actually, my uncle's a well-known surgeon and I suppose this might have been an early subconscious influence on me. Everyone in the family was always very deferential towards Uncle Harold, and Mum and Dad are always boasting about him to our friends. So I certainly grew up thinking that being in the medical profession makes you popular and admired and it must be better than slaving away in an office – especially as I've never been terribly interested in business.'

'You're being too modest,' Juliette chipped in. 'Naomi sailed through her exams, Ivor, and won a state scholoarship to medical school.'

'No regrets, I take it?' said Ivor. 'The reason I ask is that a good friend of mine from school always wanted to be a doctor, oh, from the time he was about ten years old. Funny thing is though, he won a place at Guys Hospital but gave it up after a year. He had decided that he didn't want to be a doctor after all because, now this sounds funny, he didn't like people enough to care about them.'

'Students drop out more frequently than you think,' said Naomi. 'After all, I'm in my fourth year now and we're still learning. It's easy to see that in a hospital rather than in general practice, you're involved in making life and death decicions and sometimes you know that however hard you try you're going to lose. I think that's why hospital staff tend to be people who live for the day and fight shy of long-term commitments.'

At this point Bob Jackson ambled into the bar and, after hospitably offering another round of drinks and a few minutes' desultory conversation, he and Juliette made their farewells. 'So you fight shy of long term commitments too?' asked Ivor, reverting the conversation back to her comment before Bob Jackson came in.

'I've no commitments,' replied Naomi promptly. 'And I don't think I can have any until I become a doctor in three years time. Mind, that doesn't mean I live in purdah like those women in India who are totally secluded from male company – well, you couldn't be in a hospital anyway, not with all the hanky panky between the doctors and nurses.'

'Do you know, I've always wondered about that aspect

of hospital life – is it true that doctors and nurses play around like aircraft captains and stewardesses?'

Naomi smiled and shrugged her shoulders as she finished her gin and tonic. 'There's a lot of fooling around and it's not surprising when you come to think about it – you've got men and women working closely together on important work. I don't mind telling you that the hospital I was at last year in North London seemed to have an exceptionally randy group of junior doctors. There was a chap there, Dr Jonathan, who must have gone through the entire nurses' home as well as most of the medical students!

'I'll confess something to you, Ivor,' she continued, moving herself across to sit closely by his side. 'I rather like watching a couple having sex, it turns me on. Not many girls admit to that but I don't see anything wrong in it. And you only had to be near Dr Jonathan especially when he worked on nights to know that you could come across him fucking a nurse almost anywhere. I remember one particular night shift, it was very late, well past midnight when the ward sister asked me to put some things in the laundry room for her. I walked quietly through the laundry which was tucked away from the ward and could only be reached through a narrow corridor. Well, you'd hardly credit it but in the corridor leading to the laundry there was a trail of clothes, a shirt, a pair of trousers, some underpants, a bra and a slip – I knew that these clothes hadn't fallen out of a bag of garments sent to the laundry for washing!

'Sure enough, they belonged to the randy Dr Jonathan and his friend who had been so eager to screw that they hadn't even bothered to shut themselves away! I could hear groans and squeals coming from behind the half-open door. I peered round and saw the dirty doctor lying naked on his back sporting an enormous erection and an equally nude well-built coloured nurse who I'd never seen before, standing astride him on the mattress they must have dragged in from the stores. She was just about to lower herself on his colossal cock, so I couldn't tear my eyes away as she took his throbbing tool in her hand. As she sank down on his prick, I could hear the squelchy, sucking sound as his cock pushed its way up her dripping pussy. Soon she was bouncing around and letting out little yelps as he reached up with his hands and started to tweak her nipples as he jerked his hips upwards to let his cock ream out every recess of her honeypot.

'When she felt he was about to come, she heaved herself off him and stuck her ample bum out for him to fuck her doggie-style. He took hold of his gleaming cock and humped himself over her, cupping her breasts in his hands as he spurted his jism inside her sopping slit.

'They hadn't noticed me and I was now feeling so worked up that I rushed off to the spare room and brought myself off with my fingers, biting my knuckle so that I wouldn't make any noise. I hid in there until they both went out. Later, Dr Jonathan came sidling up to me and said: "I hope you enjoyed the performance – what about taking part next time? It's much more fun!" The so-and-so had seen me at the door but, as he had said to me, he didn't want to embarrass Nurse Bristow so he had carried on regardless.'

Ivor finished his drink and said: 'I've heard of people saying thank you for coming, doctor but this is ridiculous!'

Naomi laughed heartily and said: 'I must remember that, but the truth is that Dr Jonathan and I never actually made it together – though we did get quite close once or twice!'

'Tell me about it over dinner,' said Ivor, rising from his chair. 'I thought we'd have an early meal and then take in a film.'

'I'd love some dinner,' she said as she also got up from her chair. 'I didn't even have time for a sandwich at lunch and all I've had since breakfast is a biscuit and three cups of tea. I'm sure that's why those gins loosened my tongue so quickly – really, I shouldn't have told you such a rude story about Doctor Jonathan.'

'Please don't apologise, I thoroughly enjoyed hearing all about him,' said Ivor cheerfully. 'Now, did Juliette tell you that I'd booked a table at the Yangste?' She nodded and said: "Sounds scrumptious, but can we save the film for another time? I have to start work at six thirty tomorrow morning and I don't want a late night."

'Sure,' said Ivor, gliding his way through the thickening crowd of drinkers round the bar. 'I've also got a heavy schedule tomorrow,' he fibbed, thinking of the procession of Leon Standlake's girls who would be coming into his office eager to please as they auditioned for his work.

A light patter of spring rain had begun to fall but Ivor only had to wait a minute before he hailed a passing taxi which screeched to a stop outside the pub. 'I don't usually take the car in to work,' he explained, 'though if I had known I was to have the pleasure of seeing you I would have got Juliette to feed the meters for me. But we can get a cab back to my flat after dinner and I'll take you home. Do you live near Juliette?'

'No, I share a flat with two other girls in Chalk Farm.'

'Great! I'm only in West Hampstead so that's no problem at all,' said Ivor. He was pleased about this because he didn't want to take Naomi back home in a cab from the restaurant which would give him neither time nor the opportunity for a lengthy good-night kiss! On the other hand, he honestly didn't fancy driving all the way to West London after the meal and a taxi ride back to his car from Soho. By then they'd both be far too tired to do anything but say bye-bye before he would have to turn the car round and come straight home!

As ever, the food at Yangtse was delicious. They both tucked into steaming hot plates of sweet and sour chicken, beef chop suey and egg fried rice. They chatted animatedly and very quickly the magnetic connection between two sexually attracted people was firmly in position. Ivor's hands trembled as he lifted his cup of Chinese tea to his mouth as he imagined the luscious girl's breasts falling out of the confines of her bra and into his waiting palms. Over the tablecloth it crossed Naomi's mind how wonderful it would be to lunge across, kiss Ivor long and wet and wrap her hands around his thick, pulsing cock and ravish him.

Although nothing was said, they exchanged heated glances across the table and Naomi slipped off her shoe and moved a stockinged foot up between Ivor's legs under the cover of the tablecloth. She felt the meaty bulge of his shaft with her toes and with a wicked smile he began to grind his groin against her foot. As luck would have it, Ivor was wearing the fashionable no-lace slip-on shoes so he was also able to insinuate a sock covered foot under Naomi's short skirt. She squeezed it between her thighs as she felt his toes insinuate themselves against her dampening crotch.

'How about a dessert? Some lychees or would you like one of those sticky little Chinese sweets?' invited Ivor gently when the waiter appeared to clear the dishes, his voice belying the fact that his prick was threatening to burst through the lightweight material of his suit.

'Nothing more, thank you,' murmured Naomi with a tiny 'ouf' as Ivor's big toe traced the length of her crack underneath her moist little panties. She agreed immediately to his suggestion that they took coffee at Ivor's flat.

They settled back and relaxed, leaning against each other in the dark corner of the cab as the driver headed north along Charing Cross Road. Naomi smelled Ivor's expensive after-shave and her eyes focused on his hand resting on the seat. Her face flushed as she imagined how nice it would be if those long fingers were sliding in and out of her wet pussy. Ivor's mind was running on a parallel track for his hand began a slow, sensual massage of her thigh. She did not draw away but instead arched her back and pressed even closer to him. Massaging gently but steadily he worked his way to the front of her leg and slipped his hand under her mini skirt. She spread her legs for him which caused the skirt to ride up even further, showing the tops of her black stockings. As the taxi sped through the light traffic along Hampstead Road his fingers lightly caressed her pussy lips before rolling down her panties over her hips.

'Ivor, are you sure he can't see us?' whispered Naomi, jerking her head towards the driver. 'No way, not over on this side,' he replied softly and pulled her knickers down over her thighs. Now he pressed his forefinger directly into her squishy pussy as he bent down to kiss her and her arms came up to his back, pressing lightly. He kissed her softly, making it last long enough to become significant and then pulled away gently before returning to her mouth more urgently, saying nothing as he looked into the deep liquid submission of her warm, brown eyes.

He stroked the pouting lips of her cunt, playing and teasing with her curly pubic hair. Then she pushed her pussy against his hand to increase the pleasure he was giving her and in response he began to rub harder.

'Oooh, that's nice,' she gasped as the heat between her legs reached boiling point. Ivor slipped one and then two fingers inside her wet crack, his long, sensitive fingers groping deep inside her, finding her most hidden nooks and making her shudder all over as their tongues worked frantically inside each other's mouths. The trembling girl shivered again with desire and started to moan so loudly that Ivor brought his other hand round to her lips to muffle the sound. But she continued to whimper with passion as he stroked inside her churning love channel, finding her erect, rubbery clitty and making circles around it, finger-fucking her faster and faster and using his thumb to massage the twitching, protruding sex organ.

'Please, Ivor, please,' she whispered, not even sure what she was asking for as he continued to stroke and caress her as her hips jerked up and down, pushing, pushing, pushing, pushing against his hand. The tangy aroma which emanated from her excited pussy now pervaded the taxi and the seat was wet and slippery from her juices. If the driver had turned his head or if anyone else had come into the cab just then, neither Naomi nor Ivor would have cared for they could not have stopped even if they had wanted to.

She grabbed hold of his straining cock and he was so carried away by now that he unzipped his fly and her hand plunged in and pulled out his enormous stiff prick. She squeezed the throbbing shaft as Ivor's hand became a blur as he built up his finger-fucking to a glorious climax. Her legs were spread wide, her thighs now gleaming with her juices until with a throaty sigh she came in a sudden release, clamping her thighs together round his hand. Ever so slowly she came back to earth and then, still holding his engorged rock hard cock in her grasp, she jerked her hand up and down the smooth skinned shaft, faster and faster until seconds later a sticky fountain of white jism flooded out over his helmet and down over her hand. 'Aaargh!' he groaned as she continued to manipulate his pulsing cock until he was milked dry.

Naomi rummaged in her handbag for a tissue whilst Ivor reached inside his jacket pocket for a handkerchief. 'We're almost here,' said Ivor as the taxi swung left off Finchley Road and into Compagne Gardens. He was busy zipping up his fly while Naomi decided to kick off her panties completely and stuffed them inside her handbag. When the taxi stopped outside Barnicoat Mansions they got out and Ivor added a generous tip to the fare. As he pulled out the keys to his flat, an elderly man came out of the block. Ivor recognised him as Mr Cohen who lived with his wife in the apartment below his own, and he shouted at the taxi driver to wait for him. Ivor held open the door until he arrived and Mr Cohen beamed at him. 'Thank you, Ivor, I never thought I'd get a cab at the front door at this time of night but I've got to dash down to the all night chemist in Golders Green to get this prescription for Betty. Her asthma's playing her up again.

'You just come back from a night up West? Good luck to you,' he said as Ivor helped him into the cab. 'Cor blimey, what a pong in here. You been to Billingsgate fish market this evening, driver?' he asked as Ivor hastily took the giggling Naomi's arm and he hustled her up the drive as quickly as possible.

Once safely inside his flat Ivor saw that the wheel of fortune was continuing to spin in his direction. Mrs Dawson had been in a day early and the apartment sparkled like a new pin. 'How bright and clean you keep your pad, Ivor,' said Naomi admiringly as she looked at the shining surfaces and spotless carpets. 'I hate men who live like utter slobs. You certainly put several friends of mine to shame. Did you spend last night cleaning up after a hectic weekend?

'One does one's best,' said Ivor shamelessly as he poured some cognac and handed Naomi the very same goblet from which Alison had drunk the night before! She sipped and then said suddenly: 'It's warm in here, isn't it? Do you mind if I pop into your bedroom and change into something more comfortable?'

Ivor grinned wolfishly and shook his head. 'Be my guest,' he replied, 'and meanwhile I'll put on some music.' He ripped off his tie and kicked off his shoes before switching on the stereo and pulling out a Duke Ellington album from the pile of records neatly stacked on the floor. As the mellow music floated out from the speakers the door to the bedroom opened and Naomi came into the room. Ivor looked up and caught his breath for the exquisite girl was standing stark naked in the doorway. Slowly she moved towards him and not for the first time in his life, Ivor gloried at the sight of the exquisite beauty afforded by the nude body of a pretty young woman. What a wonderful creation the female form is, he marvelled as his eyes roved greedily over the swell of her large, globular breasts and the taut raspberry nipples that looked slightly away from each other. They acted as magical magnets to his hands as she walked steadily towards him. He looked down at her dark, thickly bushed pussy and when she pressed herself to him they

94

reeled drunkenly back to the bedroom where he kissed and sucked on her erect nipples, tugging at them with his teeth as she tugged at buttons and zips and in under a minute Ivor too was naked, his swollen cock squashed delightedly between their bellies as they rolled around together, their mouths crushed together as their hands and fingers patted and petted, caressed and stroked as shivers of desire racked through them both.

But Naomi withdrew, pushed Ivor upon his back, and half sat up before slipping herself down the bed until her lips reached the bared knob of Ivor's quivering cock. She tongued his helmet, washing the mushroom dome and running over the tiny eye to catch a sticky drop of pre-cum that had already formed there. Then she opened her mouth and sucked in half his shaft, closing her lips firmly around the hot, soft skin of his tool. She was rewarded by a sigh of sheer ecstasy from the back of Ivor's throat as she let her head rise and fall and he pressed his hand on her head, pressing it downwards as she sucked vigorously on his pulsating prick, working her pink tongue round his twitching tool and running her teeth up and down the veiny shaft which seemed to grow even harder in her mouth.

'God, I'm coming,' panted Ivor and this made her gobble his cock at a frantic pace whilst she gently squeezed his hairy ballsack. A throaty growl escaped from Ivor's lips as his body went rigid and he orgasmed with a huge upwards jerk of his hips, sending great jets of warm, frothy spunk in Naomi's mouth. She swallowed his semen with relish, determined to milk every last droplet of jism from his still semi-erect penis. She freed his cock from between her lips and squeezed her ample breasts together, stuffing his still stiff shaft into the valley between her bosoms. Ivor cried out in ecstasy as he spurted the last jet of spunk and she smeared the sticky jism all round her dark red saucer-shaped aureoles.

They lay there for some minutes, letting the haunting, sensual sounds of Duke Ellington's music wash over them. 'You know something, Ivor, I would imagine there must be a queue of women waiting to be bedded by you,' said Naomi lazily.

'Now there's a happy thought – but what makes you propound such a wild diagnosis, doctor?' replied Ivor, running his fingers inside the wet, silky strands of her pubic bush.

She kissed him lightly on the cheek. 'You know how to drive a woman wild. There aren't many men who know how to do that, even though it isn't all that difficult. It's important to know just when a girl is in the mood for a fuck and you really know how to turn on your partner – lots of cuddles and kisses and plenty of patient foreplay. I can tell from the way we made love that you're a guy who genuinely believed that my satisfaction was as important as your own. Also, you don't make the common mistakes that turn women off. Do you know what those are?'

'No, but you're going to tell me and I'll take notes to make sure that I don't make any of these mistakes in the future!'

Naomi smiled and said: "Well, for starters, I'm sure you don't go wham, bam, thank you ma'am and then turn over and fall asleep!'

'N-o-o, I try not to,' he said hesitatingly. 'But on the other hand, it's fair to say that energy levels rise and fall more dramatically for boys during love-making. After orgasm, we're basically knackered! When I was sixteen I could fuck again almost immediately after coming, but now I need some time to recuperate.'

'Fair enough, but a girl still wants to feel close and wanted. You feel rejected or used if, after you've fucked, he simply rolls off, turns his back and begins snoring.'

Ivor nodded his agreement and kissed her deliciously rubbery nipple before saying: 'Yes, I can appreciate how awful that could make a girl feel and only the most selfish male chauvinist pig would behave like that. But girls can be just as tactless, Naomi. I remember when I was at college, I was doing a summer job in a petrol station and I really fancied Tracey, the girl at the cash desk. One night she let me take her to the pub and on the way home we had a quick knee-trembler at the side of her parents' house. At first she didn't want to but then she sighed and said: "Oh, all right then, if you must . . ." and whilst I was pumping away she said in a bored tone: "Haven't you finished yet?"'

'What a turn-off! But I can't stand marathon men myself so I have a tiny grain of sympathy for Tracey – though speed merchants are just as bad. What else don't I like now? Oh yes, men who have to ask "how was it for you?" For heaven's sake, if they really can't tell if I've come or not they should be celibate!'

'What a terrible thought.' Ivor shuddered and, as if to blanket out such a fearful fate, he kissed her breasts and slid a questing finger between her pussy lips.

Naomi turned and said with a twinkle: 'Ivor, are you thinking about a little fuck?'

'It certainly crossed my mind,' he admitted, taking hold of his stiffening cock and placing it in her hand. She eagerly grasped his erect penis and rubbed the swollen shaft up and down until it pulsed and twitched between her fingers. And then with a giggle: 'Oh dear, and there I was thinking about a big one!'

'You rude thing, I've a good mind to smack your botty for being so cheeky,' Ivor admonished the saucy young vixen, who was now squeezing his rigid member with both her hands.

'Promises, promises – wow, wow, wow!' she squealed, letting go of Ivor's veiny truncheon as he pulled her face down over his knees and smoothed his hand over the cool, velvet-like skin of her luscious backside. She turned her head and said with a smile: 'I wouldn't mind a nice little spanking, Ivor. Not too hard though.'

He was only too delighted to oblige and gently smacked her beautiful bottom. With each slap she opened her legs slightly and Ivor could see the wrinkled little rosette of her bum hole winking at him. Naomi wriggled and winced as a pink blush appeared on the plump white globes of her buttocks as they jiggled under his hand. 'Oooh! That'll do, I'm tingling all over, finish me off now with your nice big cock.'

Ivor rolled her back onto the mattress and knelt between her thighs, and holding his bursting erection in his hand, nudged the tip of the bared helmet between her pouting, wet pussy lips. 'Put it inside me, please,' she whispered, bracing herself for the onslaught. Slowly but firmly he eased his shaft inside her clinging love channel and before he even began to begin thrusting backwards and forwards she shuddered uncontrollably, her love juices flowing freely over his excited shaft. Then he started to fuck her, pistoning his pulsating prick to and fro, faster. She clasped her legs over his back as he buried his cock in her hot, juicy cunt. They could both hear the erotic squelching as his prick slid in and out of her love-box and the slip slap sound of his ballsack bouncing against her bottom.

'I'm coming, darling, come with me, over the top, aaah, aaaah,' Naomi screamed out as he bore down on her, his muscular frame now soaked with perspiration, fucking harder and harder with the rippling movement of his shaft sending electric shocks of delight along the twitching walls of her sweet honeypot.

The pair melted into a torrent of mutual orgasm as, with one final lunge, they came together with great cries as Ivor shot a tremendous stream of spunk into her sopping sheath. Their bodies slithered against each other as they writhed in the passionate throes of ecstacy until, sated by their frenzied pleasure, they slumped down in an erotic tangle of naked limbs.

Naomi kissed his ear and whispered: 'Darling, I hate to mention it but I did tell you that I've got this dreadful early start tomorrow and it's already past midnight.'

'Oh no, I'd quite forgotten,' groaned Ivor, pulling a pillow over his head. 'But why can't you stay the night and I'll run you to the hospital first thing in the morning. I was going to take my car to town anyway so it would be no trouble.'

'No can do, I'm afraid,' she said regretfully. 'I must change my clothes and anyhow I have to pick up some stuff from home first. Sorry Ivor, but I'd better leave now. Honestly, there's nothing I'd like better than to stay but it'll have to be another time.'

'Okay,' he said resignedly. 'We'd better get up straight-away as it'll only be harder to wake up in the morning. It won't take more than five minutes to drive to your flat.

'Last one to finish dressing is a cissy!' he added, jumping out of bed as he playfully smacked her quivering bottom.

'Not fair, all you need to do is to slip on pants, shirt, trousers, socks and shoes,' Naomi complained. 'Look at all the bits and pieces I've got to put on.'

Nevertheless, in less than five minutes they were out of the flat and Ivor was turning his car round to zoom up towards Chalk Farm, where Naomi shared a ground floor apartment with two other girls. 'Are either of them medical students too?' asked Ivor, putting his foot down on the accelerator and flicking his eyes up to the mirror to make sure that the vehicle behind was not a police car on the prowl.

'No, Sheila's an assistant editor at some highbrow publishing house and young Babs works for Iain Wiggins as his personal secretary.'

'What, not the dashing young merchant adventurer as the gossip columnists always seem to label him? The man who always has a different girl on his arm at every premiere and posh party reported in the papers and is always rumoured to be shortly announcing his engage-ment.'

'The very same – but despite what you read, Babs tells me that he's no Casanova. Far from it, in fact, as Babs is pretty sure that he's a woofter and the poor chap pays God knows how much for girls to chaperone him as he's terrified of coming out of the closet.'

'Oh well, it takes all sorts, I suppose, though I'll never understand why girls don't turn them on. Still, live and let live especially as it means less competition for crumpet!' On Naomi's direction, he slowed down and pulled up to a halt outside the large house which, like others in the tree-lined avenue, had been converted into flats. She peered out of the car and said: 'I'm surprised the light's still on – Sheila's away on some course or other and Babs is usually in bed by this time.'

'I'll come in with you just to make sure all is well,' Ivor insisted before Naomi could say any more. He took her arm and guided her up the steps. She opened the front door and hurried through the door of her flat and turned the key in the lock.' Babs, are you alright?' she called out as a cheery voice replied: 'Hi, Naomi, yes, of course all's well. How did your evening go, love?'

'Very nicely thank you,' Naomi called back and her flatmate sauntered into the hallway from the lounge. Babs had obviously expected Naomi to be alone for the stunning tall girl was wearing only a transparent baby-doll nightie through which Ivor could see her large, uptilted breasts and the thick fleece of hair between the tops of her long legs.

'Oh, my God, I didn't know we had company, I'll be back in a jiffy,' gasped Babs as she fled into her bedroom. Ivor grinned and called after her: 'It's alright, don't worry, I'm not wearing my glasses.'

Naomi looked puzzled. 'But you don't wear specs, Ivor,' she said with a frown. 'No, but Babs don't have to know that!' he rejoined. Naomi giggled as Babs came back, tying the belt of a towelling robe around her waist. 'How embarrassing,' she laughed though Ivor noted with approval that she wasn't as mortified as might be expected at having a strange young man see her naked body.

'That makes a fitting end to the evening, and serves me right, I suppose,' laughed the dazzling auburn-haired girl. 'I've been rather naughty and if you like I'll tell you both a funny story – after you've introduced me to this gentleman, Naomi.'

'Ivor, this is Babs Gardener. Babs, meet Ivor Belling.' said Naomi and Ivor detected just the tiniest edge of frost in her voice. Well, hell's teeth, he thought, I might also be a wee bit put out if the boot were on the other foot and I had just brought a new girl-friend into my flat and the first thing she sees is a good looking young fellow.

So Ivor made a point of wrapping his left arm round Naomi whilst he shook hands with Babs. 'I'd just put the kettle on, would you like some coffee?' she asked and Ivor hesitated. 'It's a bit late and –'

'Oh come on, be a sport, I'm dying to tell somebody,' she chuckled. 'What happened to me tonight was so interesting that I feel like a character in that old joke about Hymie Goldberg rushing into a Catholic Church and grabbing hold of the priest coming out of the confessional. "Father, Father," he shouts. "An hour ago I bumped into a gorgeous young blonde outside the Church who pulled me into the woods and we made mad passionate love three times without stopping – and I'm fifty seven years old!"

'"Why in heaven's name are you telling me all this, Hymie? You're not even a Catholic!" "Sorry, Father," says Hymie very apologetically. "But I just had to tell someone!"'

Ivor burst out laughing and turned to Naomi. Her good temper had rapidly returned as soon as she felt Ivor's arm round her waist, reassuring her that there was no cause for her to be jealous of her sexy room-mate. 'Do you mind if I stay to hear Babs's story, Naomi?' he said. 'If it's anything like her joke it should be well worth hearing.'

'What the heck, it's already so late that another half hour won't make much difference,' said Naomi good humouredly, moving towards the kitchen. 'Come on, I'll make us all a hot drink. Coffee as usual for you, Babs, I suppose. I'm going to have tea. What about you, Ivor?'

'I'll have the same, one big sugar, please,' said Ivor

absently, for his attention was centred on Babs. She had shown him into the lounge and curled herself up in an armchair, tucking her legs underneath her. This loosened the belt of her robe and the front of it divided, showing that Babs had taken off the nightie she had been wearing when Ivor and Naomi had entered. Under the robe she was quite nude.

Perhaps it's for the best, thought Ivor, as she rearranged the robe so that he had only a fleeting glimpse of the generously sized hairy triangle between her legs. He smiled glassily at her as Naomi came in with a tray on which stood three mugs proclaiming the glories of Tottenham Hotspur Football Club. 'I don't know if I can drink from one of those,' said Ivor in mock indignation. 'Not after what the Spurs did to my team on Saturday.'

'Oh dear, are you a Fulham fan, Ivor?' said Naomi. 'You have all my sympathy, you poor thing. Five-one at home, wasn't it? These mugs come from my brother, he's a Spurs fanatic like my father though I've been a Chelsea supporter myself ever since he took me to Spurs back in 1957 to the first game of the season. It was the first time Jimmy Greaves played in Chelsea's first team. I'll never forget how he left Danny Blanchflower sitting on his bottom in the penalty area and slotted in an equaliser. He was the greatest footballer I've ever seen, but I think he's too much of an individualist for the England team.'

'Gosh, you sound like a real fan,' said Ivor, taking a mug from the tray.

Naomi nodded her head. 'I love football,' she said. 'I go to every home game I can get to and I just hope I'll be able to see some of the World Cup matches next year.'

Babs took her mug of coffee and giggled: 'I can't say I like football very much, though Iain has a season ticket at West Ham. I think he'd give anything to meet that handsome blond man who's captain of the England team. What's his name now, I've forgotten it.'

'Bobby Moore,' supplied Ivor, who could now see that the girl was, if not actually drunk, was certainly three sheets in the wind. 'So Iain Wiggins is a woofter, Babs? You'd never guess it from his press cuttings.'

She shook her head. 'No, you wouldn't, would you? But at least I found out tonight that Larry, his best friend, swings both ways. Larry's only twenty six and I've often wondered whether he was really one hundred per cent homosexual although he's sharing a house with Iain out in Letchmore Heath in Hertfordshire. Well, he has a small flat fifty yards away from Iain's place but that's just a front. So when Larry came to the office tonight to leave some papers for Iain to sign – Iain's been in America for the last four days and was due back at Heathrow some time tonight – I deliberately gave him the treatment when he came out of Iain's office. "I've been working late and now my dinner date's telephoned to cancel. What a swizz!" I wailed and Larry shot me an old-fashioned look. "Is this your regular boy friend?" he asked and I told him that I didn't have a serious fella in tow at the moment. Anyhow, he fell for the bait and asked me to have dinner with him. We went to the Auberge and then Larry was going to drive me back here. But as we climbed into his MG – which had been a birthday present from Iain, incidentally – I said: "Oh, damn it, Larry, I've left the Goldhill files at Iain's house. He's not coming to the office tomorrow but I need it first thing. Could you be a love and drive me over there before taking me home?"

' "Of course I can," he said gallantly and as we drove out of London I let my hand rest on his thigh as I leaned against him. By the time we arrived at Iain's, my hand was gently resting in Larry's lap though I couldn't feel whether he'd got a hard-on or not. Well, we got out the car but instead of walking to the front door I guided Larry round to the side of the house and into the back garden. It was very dark but there were a couple of lights on upstairs. As Iain was away a great deal he had time switches fixed throughout the house, so the fact that the bedroom light was on didn't necessarily mean that Iain had returned from the airport.

'I pulled Larry towards one of the big trees in the garden and pressed him against the trunk. I kissed him firmly on the lips and at first he simply stood there, perhaps bewildered by this sudden show of passion. But when I forced my tongue between his lips he responded quickly enough and he crushed me in his arms as we french kissed like mad. My hand stole down to squeeze his cock but there seemed to be little stirring around there. Obviusly it was the shock, I decided, and so I wriggled out of his arms and moved slightly to the side. I unhooked my skirt, letting it fall to the ground. I stepped out of it and then quickly tugged down my tights and panties together and leaned back against the tree and started to stroke my fleecy pussy. "Wouldn't you like to fuck me, Larry?" I cooed invitingly as I continued to frig myself, fingering my pussy and playing with my clitty as I felt myself getting all moist.

'He didn't answer but instead looked frantically up to the light upstairs in the house and I also glanced up and saw the shape of a man silhouetted against the window. It had to be Iain and the idea of my poofy boss watching me as I brought myself off made me feel even randier.

'I stroked myself faster and faster, feeling myself getting hotter and wetter. Then, with a hoarse cry, Larry suddenly turned to me and plastered his lips over mine. His hands came up to play with my tits and I unzipped his flies to take out his now stiffening cock. I pulled down his trousers and rubbed his swollen shaft up and down until it was as hard as rock. I guided his blunt, fleshy knob against my love lips and then he jerked forward and began fucking me, ramming his shaft deep into my cunt. I felt an orgasm building up inside of me, getting stronger and stronger and when I felt his prick spasm inside me I finally let go. I came just as he drenched my pussy with a fierce fountain of jism and we rocked backwards and forwards in a gloriously spontaneous fuck which left us weak kneed and exhausted but very, very happy.

'After he caught his breath Larry kissed me again and told me how great it was. I said: "Well, I enjoyed it too, Larry," and we burst out laughing. "That must have made a nice change," I said and Larry nodded. "You can say that again," he complained. "Iain overlooks the man in me completely. He takes me from behind and treats me like a woman. He'll make a real fairy out of me if he can but I still like some pussy now and then despite all of Iain's efforts."

'He whirled round as we heard footsteps approaching us. It was Iain, dressed in pyjamas and a dressing gown though he had slipped on a pair of tennis shoes. "Ah, just as I thought," he said and, taking hold of Larry's cock, began to manipulate his shaft until it began to stretch and thicken and his beautiful round knob was uncovered as his foreskin snapped back. Iain dropped to his knees and started to suck the throbbing prick which bobbed up in front of his face. He lathered his tongue around Larry's swollen prick. His head moved upward and downward, forward and backward to increase the sensual pleasure for them both. Iain shot me a look of triumph as he continued to palate Larry's wonderful cock. But I was determined not to be outdone so I crawled between Larry's legs and began to lick his hairy balls, feeding my growing appetite for him. But Iain was determined that Larry should come in his mouth and, with a convulsive jerk, he obliged, sending a stream of spunk down Iain's throat. He gulped it down with evident relish as he glared at me with a glint of anger in his eyes.

'After Larry withdrew his shrunken penis Iain said to me with a vicious smile: "Are you satisfied now, Babs? Larry's mine and I intend to keep things that way. Don't bother going into the office tomorrow, you're fired. I'll send your wages on to your home address."

'I just stood there flabbergasted and my jaw dropped. I think I might have burst into tears but Larry said fiercely: "Don't be such a shit, Iain! Babs is a marvellous secretary and anything personal that takes place outside the office is nothing to do with you. If she goes, I go and I might go straight to the Sunday newspapers as well." My boss paled at this threat and pursed his lips. "Are you blackmailing me?" he said, aghast at the thought of seeing his name splashed over the front pages of *The People* or the *News Of The World*.

'"No, because I don't want money. But you can consider it a threat if you like, I don't care," said Larry bravely. Iain considered the situation and said: "Well, perhaps I was a little hasty but I love you, Larry, and I don't like the idea of sharing. However, how about leaving matters as if this evening's unfortunate little contretemps never actually occurred? We'll forget all about it. How does that sound?"

'"Much, much better, and I'll reward you in the way you like best," said Larry happily. "Now Babs is such a conscientious girl that she came here tonight to pick up the Goldhill files. So let me give them to her, run her back home and when I come back I hope you'll have made the bed and have something nice and warm for me to slip into." I was tempted to say that to fulfil his wishes, Iain should stick his bum into the oven but I bit my tongue and simply looked smugly at my boss as he nodded his head in agreement.

'And that's all, folks! Quite an extraordinary evening, don't you agree?' She sat back, curled up in her chair like a sleek, sexy kitten.

Ivor moved round in his chair and his elbow sent his mug crashing to the floor. 'Oh, fuck it!' he swore softly and immediately apologised but Babs hastened to put him at ease. 'Don't worry, it's not broken.'

'Well, actually I was apologising for my bad language,' said Ivor which made Naomi giggle. 'We hear that word all the time in hospital. My friend Terri says the English wouldn't be able to communicate without it. After all, you just used fuck as an expression of dismay, *oh, fuck it*.'

'Yes, and you can use it as an expression of displeasure, *what the fuck is going on?*' said Babs.

Ivor now warmed to the game. 'Or how about confusion, *what the fuck?*' Now Naomi took up the reins. 'Don't forget disapproval, *he's a fucking dickhead!*' Babs was not to be outdone. 'Chalk up despair, *this is a fine fucking mess,*' she suggested.

Naomi thought for a moment and said: 'Then there's the inquest into what went wrong like *Fulham were fucked by the lack of a decent defence.*'

'So true,' agreed Ivor ruefully. 'As in plain, simple aggression, *Fuck you!* or the philosophical, *who gives a fuck?*'

'But the best of all is the original verb,' cried Babs, climbing to her feet and shucking off her robe to stand thrillingly naked in the centre of the room. 'As in *who's game for a good fuck?*'

Ivor licked his lips but he first looked across at Naomi. She met his gaze and said: 'I don't object at all, Ivor, honestly I don't, but if it's OK with you let's make it a threesome.'

'By all means,' he replied, unbuttoning his shirt. 'Let's all go to my room,' suggested Babs, where the girls sat Ivor on a chair as Babs helped Naomi undress and the two girls leaped naked upon Babs's bed. Naomi tweaked up Babs's tawny nipples to a fine erection as the aroused teenager grasped Naomi's bum cheeks and fondled and squeezed them voluptuously. Babs laid Naomi on the bed and began sucking on her huge red titties as she pulled apart the trembling Naomi's inner thighs, giving Ivor a grandstand view of the pink, pouting cunt lips upon which Babs quickly placed her hand and began to finger fuck the whimpering girl. Babs now moved herself round so that her body was straddled over her partner until her own gorgeously rounded bottom was directly over Naomi's mouth. She continued to finger fuck Naomi as she gently lowered her bum so that Naomi could cup her fleshy buttocks in her hands and insert her tongue inside the pink folds of her quivering sex chink. She craned her head forward to dive into Naomi's curly black muff to complete

107

a sensuous *soixante neuf* which so excited the watching Ivor that, almost unknowingly, his hand strayed down to his tremendous stiffstander. He began to frig himself as the girls licked and lapped each other, probing, sucking and rubbing their cracks and making each other shriek with pleasure as they shuddered to a glorious mutual climax.

The girls continued to play with each other, grinding their cunts together. Then Babs climbed on top of Babs and rubbed herself off on Naomi's back, raising her buttocks and opening her legs so that Ivor could see her prominent pussy. She turned her head round and called out: 'Come on, Ivor, what are you waiting for? Don't waste that fine-looking stiffie by playing with yourself!' Ivor shot up from his chair and positioned himself behind Babs as Naomi rolled out from underneath her. The teenage girl reached round and placed his bare knob in the cleft between her plump, rounded buttocks. Naomi suddenly reappeared with a pot of cold cream in her hand. 'Take your cock out for a moment, Ivor,' she commanded and as if in a dream Ivor obeyed. She smeared the cream all over his pulsing prick and with a wicked little smile, whispered: 'Babs likes it up the bum, you know, but it's much nicer that way if you grease your cock first.

'Very thoughtful,' gasped Ivor as he pulled open Babs' unresisting bum cheeks and aimed his cock towards the wrinkled little brown orifice. He pushed forward and with only a short cry of discomfort from the girl, his cock was firmly lodged in Bab's warm, tight bottom. To their mutual delight, he began to work himself backwards and forwards with vigour, making Babs' bum cheeks smack against his belly as she cried out again, this time with delight: 'A-h-r-e, a-h-r-e, keep going, that's the ticket, slide home you lovely big-cocked boy!'

Ivor screwed up his eyes in sheer bliss and then leaned forward to fondle her luscious, hanging breasts and play with her giant, erect tawny nipples. He thrust his hips forward so powerfully that the full length of his twitching tool was absorbed in her bum. 'Babs, I'm not hurting you, am I?' he said anxiously.

For answer she waggled her bottom provocatively and lifted her head from the pillow. Ivor was relieved to see that there was no doubt of her complete and total enjoyment of the sensation of his thick prick pounding in and out of her bottom.

He needed no further urging when she gasped, 'Now, Ivor, now!' and almost immediately he flooded her arsehole with such vibrant jets of jism that he almost saw as well as felt the ripples of orgasm running down Babs's spine as she reached a magnificent climax. She wriggled her bottom again as spout after spout of creamy spunk filled her tingling hole until with a succulent 'pop' Ivor withdrew his still semi-stiff shaft and sank back on his haunches. Naomi moved up on the bed and eagerly sucked his glistening wet cock, gulping down the last drains of his emission as her hands jerked up and down his tool. Then, when she had milked his now rapidly shrinking penis of the final drops of sperm, she sat sedately back as Ivor and Babs lay panting and heaving from their exertions.

'I really am going to bed now as I still have to be up at the crack of dawn,' announced Naomi. 'But there's no point you going back to your flat till morning, Ivor. Why not sleep here with us? I promise I'll wake you in time so you'll return to your flat refreshed and raring to go to work.'

'Gosh, that's certainly a tempting invitation,' he replied as Babs stroked his limp cock which hung listlessly over his thigh. 'Yes, do stay, Ivor. I tell you what, I'll run the bath and we can all clean up before going to sleep.'

'Why not indeed,' murmured Ivor, now comfortably snuggled down with his mouth pressed against Naomi's turgid nipple and his hand snugly fitted between her legs. He only had five minutes respite for soon the still-naked Babs was shaking him awake. 'Come on, Ivor, let's have a refreshing shower,' she said, pulling him off the soft, warm body of her sleeping flatmate. Obediently, Ivor followed her into the bathroom and stood under the warm jets of water cascading down from the showerhead. He soaped himself all over and Babs's eyes focused on his muscular body and tight, dimpled buttocks. She felt her pussy moistening between her legs and said throatily: 'Ivor, switch the shower off for a moment.' He didn't hear her above the noise of the water so she stepped beside him and turned off the tap whilst with her other hand she grasped his gleaming, wet cock and rubbed it gently up to a fast thickening stiffness until it stood at its fullest height up against his belly with the uncapped knob reaching his navel. Her nipples fairly trembled with excitement at the idea of this throbbing prick crashing into her cunney and her clitty popped out of its hood, seeking further attention.

She had kept the plug in the bath so there was a slippery bedding of soapy, warm water in which they could play as their mouths mashed together. Babs sank down on her back as Ivor moved his lips from her pretty mouth to her large cork-tipped breasts. He arduously licked and slurped one hard, dark nipple up to peak erectness before switching his attentions to the other. Babs moaned gently as he moved inexorably downwards, kissing her navel, circling the tiny circle with his tongue. Then in a flash he was lapping at her juicy slit, licking every inch of her cunney lips, sucking them into his mouth before sliding his tongue into her tight, wet hole.

Babs shivered with joy as her supple young body slithered and twisted. Ivor eagerly lapped up her flowing juices, his teeth nipping unbearably at her excited clitty, his lips sucking hard as he licked deeper and deeper until she thought she would swoon from the glorious waves of ecstatic, carnal delight that emanated from her wantonly uninhibited cunt. She stayed on her back, cossetted by the warm water as Ivor's thick tool wriggled its way between her heaving breasts and into her open mouth. She clamped her lips tightly around the pulsating pole as he ran his hands over her breasts. Ivor was surprised himself by the strength of his passion and the power still surging throughout his hard, rampant prick. He eased his penis out of her mouth and slid his cock down towards her silky bush until his knob just grazed her cunney lips. Then he raised himself up on the palms of his hands and tenderly pushed foward, his knob slowly sinking in her willing cave as he buried his length inside until their hairs crunched together.

They fucked in a slow, rhythmic fashion as the water seemed to coax their bodies to new heights. Supported just on his fingertips and toes, Ivor's cock entered her pussy at a high angle and he thrust home with a violent intensity against the soft, resilient flesh of her soaking cunt from which her juices were already flowing into the bathwater. As they approached the climax Ivor changed the tempo to one of short, sharp jabs and she rotated her bottom whilst he pulsed in and out. He pumped faster and faster until with a bellow he lubricated her honeypot with a coating of sticky, white spunk. The contractions of her cunt milked his prick dry and she gripped his bum cheeks as he collapsed on top of her and they held each other close as they recovered from their exhausting but superb bout of love-making.

'It's just as well Naomi's not the jealous type,' said Ivor, levering himself up and standing up to reach for a towel. 'Because I don't think I could fuck again, not even for a knighthood and a trip round the world for myself and a friend!'

Babs sighed and pulled teasingly on his flaccid penis. 'And men have the temerity to call us the weaker sex!' she said mockingly. 'But enough's as good as a feast, so let's call it a night and go to sleep. Naomi's got a large double bed so we can both join her for a few hours' snooze. I know you two have to be back early but be a pal and let me sleep on – I don't have to be in the office till ten o'clock and I need my beauty sleep.'

'Lucky old you,' said Ivor with feeling as he wrapped

his towel round her. 'I'll be shagged out before I get to the office.'

Babs giggled and lifted her face up to kiss him on his ear. 'You can say that again, darling, because Naomi will expect you to do your duty before you get dressed in the morning.'

Ivor clapped his hand over his forehead. 'Oh no,' he groaned. 'I never thought I'd ever say this but right now all my John Thomas wants to do is wave a white flag! I tell you, Babs, it's dangerous nonsense that men have a greater sexual drive than women and it's a bloody myth that we're constantly ready and able to perform at the drop of a pair of panties!'

'I'm sure you're right,' yawned Babs. 'But it's too late for a discussion of sexual politics. Come on, tiger, let's grab some shut-eye.'

CHAPTER FOUR

Sugar and Spice

The shrill pinging of her bedside alarm clock woke Naomi
at ten minutes to six. She threw her arm out and pressed
the cancel button. The first rays of dawn illuminated the
room as she turned her naked body round and looked at
the equally nude Ivor who was still fast asleep. She
plunged her hand downwards, ran her fingers along the
length of his flaccid cock and she gave out a little sigh of
disappointment. Never mind, there isn't really time even
for a nice quickie, she consoled herself as she shook him
by the shoulder. But Ivor was sleeping so deeply that it
took Naomi a full half minute before she could shake him
awake.

'Come on, Ivor,' she whispered for she had also
promised Babs that she would try hard not to wake her
up. 'Awake! for Morning in the Bowl of Night –'

'Has flung the Stone that puts the Stars to Flight, and
Lo! the Hunter of the East has caught the Sultan's turret
in a Noose of Light,' said Ivor groggily as he stretched out
his arms and yawned, clearing his head from the last
vestiges of sleep.

'Very good, Ivor, I'm impressed,' said Naomi, giving
him a kiss. 'No need to be,' he replied. 'It just so happens
that we studied *The Rubaiyat of Omar Khayyam* at
school.

'It's good stuff though, isn't it?' he added and gave a
short laugh.

'What's so funny?' she demanded as she delightfully
massaged his neck and shoulders with her long, slender
fingers.

Ivor sat up. 'Don't you remember verse twenty eight? It

just occurred to me that it describes my situation exactly,' he said and when she shook her head he quoted: 'I came like Water and like Wind I go.'

Naomi smiled and gave his shoulders a final refreshing rub. 'We'll have to move as fast as the wind if I'm not to be late,' she said and she dragged a reluctant Ivor from between the sheets. 'There's no time and we mustn't wake Babs,' she protested as he reached out and gently pressed his hand over her curly dark thatch of pubic hair. She moved back a pace and said: 'But how about coming back tonight and I'll cook us some supper? I'm afraid you would have to make do with just me, though, as Babs is going out with a girl friend to the theatre.'

'I'd love to, thank you very much,' said Ivor warmly for, like all men, he was always extremely appreciative of any girl he had wined and dined who offered to reciprocate hospitality. He slid out of bed and they washed and dressed as quickly as possible. There was no time for breakfast but Naomi said she would be able to have some tea and toast at the hospital. They left the sleeping Babs and Ivor dropped Naomi at the Underground station.

'Come round at about half past seven tonight,' she said as he kissed her goodbye. 'And bring a toothbrush and an overnight case!' she added shamelessly at which Ivor's face creased into a large grin. He drove home and after a bath and his usual breakfast of corn flakes, toast and coffee he set out for the office.

A long queue of traffic stretched ahead of him down Avenue Road to Regents Park, moving jerkily in the bright sunshine. But Ivor was in no great hurry and he concentrated his attention on the passing women on the nearside pavement, reducing the younger and prettier girls in his mind's eye to a lush, voluptuous nudity. It was strange, he reflected, how often he could be diverted by a mane of unruly hair or the wiggling bottom of a well-filled pair of jeans only to discover when he passed by the owner of the blonde mop or the delectable buttocks, that their faces held little or no interest for him. Who looks at the mantelpiece while you're stoking the fire, his old mates at college used to say as they downed pint after pint in the students' bar after a game of football, but Ivor could never accept this. He preferred to make do with a five-knuckle shuffle rather than court a girl he did not genuinely find sexually appealing, unlike some of the other young men who boasted wildly over the number of notches on their guns. If he were ever questioned about his leg-over successes Ivor would only smile enigmatically and mutter that he preferred quality to quantity. At present, though, he was in the fortunate position of being spoiled for choice. He inched his car forward another three yards towards the traffic lights.

As the sun was now shining remarkably strongly for early Spring, Ivor decided to park the car in a side street on the edge of the parking meter zone and walk the remaining distance of just over three quarters of a mile to the office. As he strode away from the vehicle he heard a familiar voice cry out: 'Hi there, Ivor!' He looked to his right and saw walking towards him the plump figure of Cable Publicity's auditor, Harold Godfrey, who he had seen only three days before after the match on Saturday afternoon as he and Martin had walked disconsolately back from Craven Cottage.

'Hello, Harry,' said Ivor. 'You coming to see Martin this morning?'

'No, but I'm coming your way as I have to see a client only round the corner in Procter Street. Unless you want to be alone with your thoughts, we can walk to Holborn together.'

'Fine, so long as you don't want to talk about football!'

The accountant couldn't resist the temptation to make just one comment to praise his beloved Tottenham Hotspurs. 'Five-one, bit of a licking, wasn't it? Never mind, Fulham won't go down this season.'

'That's the best I think we can look forward to, not getting licked at home again like that and not going down.'

'Sounds a bit dire,' chuckled the accountant as they negotiated their way through the cars stuck in the long snarl-up that was clogging up Euston Road. 'I had a marvellous business trip to France last week with lots of licking and going down and bloody marvellous it was, old boy!'

'A marvellous business trip, you say,' echoed Ivor. 'It must have been more like monkey business from the expression on your face. I didn't think chartered accountants were allowed to fuck during business hours.'

'We're not – unless we can charge the time to a client! Seriously though, what happened was that I flew to Nice on an early-morning flight without any hassle but when I arrived I found that my hold-all had been put on a plane to Paris. Luckily, I'd kept all my papers in my briefcase which I'd kept with me but, of course, I would be without a change of clothes for the evening and the next day if the missing bag didn't turn up.

'Anyhow I reported the loss at the airline desk and I grumbled about the situation with a ground hostess and a stewardess from my flight. They were very sympathetic and they promised to find my case and send it to my hotel. More as a joke, I promised them that if they could deliver it to me later in the day, then I'd be delighted to buy them dinner.

'I took a taxi to the hotel and after registering, went to see my client who's semi-retired and lives from Easter to October in the South of France. I returned back to the hotel at about seven o'clock. As I had expected, I finished everything I had to do in one day and the idea was that I could spend the next day ambling round the town before catching the five o'clock flight back to London.

'Well, I hadn't been in five minutes when the reception called me with the news that my missing hold-all had arrived and was being sent up to my room.

'There was a knock on the door and I called out *Entrez* fully expecting to see the hotel porter. But to my surprise and delight who should come in but Lisa the ground

116

hostess and Brigitte, the stewardess. They had taken me at my word and, with a smile, Lisa claimed the meal I had promised them should they return my bag by the evening. "*C'est mon plaisir*," I said sincerely but Brigitte said: "Please speak in English, we must practice the language whenever we can and thank you for the kind invitation but we are only joking. You can buy us a drink, though, if you like."

'"No, no," I insisted. "I would love to take you both out to dinner – I'm all on my own and have nothing to do tonight." At first they demurred but in the end they accepted my invitation and we went to a lovely little bistro called La Garonne on Rue General Frederic Nolanne. What a marvellous meal, simple stuff, onion soup, bifteck and pommes frites followed by a French apple tart all washed down with two bottles of the house wine for about four quid.

'The girls insisted on buying the brandy to go with our coffee and I couldn't help remarking that it was a little odd to find such two very attractive girls without boy friends. They exchanged a brief glance and then Lisa said: "We've plenty of boy friends if and when we need them but frankly, Harry, by and large Brigitte and I far prefer each other's company." Perhaps the wine had dulled my senses for the penny hadn't dropped, so I looked at her with a puzzled expression. Brigitte could see that further explanation was needed and she said: "Harry, we are, how do you say in English, lesbians." Just my bloody luck, I thought, and my disappointment must have shown for Lisa laid a hand on my knee and let her fingers waltz up and down my thigh as she said softly: "But not exclusively, Harry, we do like to share a man from time to time. I hope we haven't shocked you too much but we do enjoy all kinds of fucking."

'Well, there's a cue if I ever heard one so I raised my glass, took a swig of brandy and said bluntly: "So do I and so there's only one question to be answered: your place or mine?" I paid the bill and walked back to the girls' flat which wasn't far away at all from my hotel. Brigitte opened a bottle of calvados and in no time at all the three of us were in the bedroom. I sat down on the bed and took off my shoes and socks. Brigitte, who was surprisingly light-skinned for a girl from the South, unbuttoned my shirt whilst the darker Lisa unclipped my belt and unzipped my trousers. I sat on the bed in my bulging Y-fronts as the girls swiftly stripped themselves naked. God, were they gorgeous, Ivor, old lad! Lisa had high, uptilted breasts, large with dark nipples with a thick, luxuriant triangle of crinkly black hair over her cunt whilst Brigitte, a strawberry blonde, also had smaller but juicy-looking firm breasts that jutted out proudly from her petite body. Her muff was sparser and I could easily make out the outline of her cunny lips through her light, wispy pubic hair.

'They lay me on the bed and pulled off my pants. My cock shot up like a guardsman on parade and Lisa lay down alongside me and without compunction started to suck my cock. Brigitte straddled me and lowered herself down so that I was able to bury my face between her soft thighs and reach her damp cunt with my mouth and fingers. I reached up and cupped her glorious breasts and rubbed her big, maroon nipples against the palms of my hands. In turn, she writhed and squirmed her honeypot even deeper inside my mouth. I wrapped one arm across her waist and grabbed her delicious bum as my lips savoured the salty flavour of her love juices.

'Lisa correctly guessed that I was on the verge of coming for she opened her mouth and my gleaming cock sprang out. She scrambled up to nibble on Brigitte's erect nipple, replacing my hand which she guided down towards her own very damp pussy and I finger fucked her whilst I managed to bring off Brigitte with my tongue. Lisa whimpered and now lay flat on her back, her long legs wide apart and I rolled over on top of her and plunged my prick inside her clinging wet love channel. We had a really wonderful fuck, nice and slow and I shafted her in long, sweeping strokes which she obviously adored. Although my lips were now firmly glued to her magnificent big tits, I could see from the corner of my eye that poor Brigitte was reduced to simply lying beside us, frantically frigging herself with her right hand stuffed between her legs. So I moved my own right hand over and replaced her fingers with my own, jerking my fingers in and out of her sopping passion pit as I continued to pump my cock in and out of Lisa's quivering quim.

'I was the first to come, sending a fierce spurt of spunk inside Lisa's cunt, and then Brigitte moaned with joy as she orgasmed and her soaking slit poured out a liberal coating of cunt juice on my fingers.'

By now Harold Godfrey and Ivor had reached Holborn and the accountant was about to cross the road into Procter Street when Ivor laid a hand on his arm. 'Don't stop there, Harry, what about poor old Lisa?'

Harold shook his head. 'Ah, well, I'm afraid that she couldn't come with a man so I retired from the fray and watched Brigitte tongue her pal up to a climax. I'm not as virile as I used to be, Ivor, but we spent the rest of the night sucking and fucking in more ways than I had thought possible. When one of us tired, the other two managed to carry on and it was past three o'clock by the time I fell asleep, nicely nestled in between the two girls. At dawn, I somehow staggered back across the road to my hotel and spent the rest of the morning in bed! As it turned out, the weather was pretty average so I didn't miss anything by not being on the promenade or on the beach. Look, next time you or Martin fancy a trip to Nice, call me and I'll give you the girls' address and telephone number.'

Ivor reached Cable Publicity's headquarters and waved politely to Tracey, the attractive new receptionist, and said good morning to Martin's secretary, the prim but efficient Miss Forsyth as he made his way to his office. Juliette was already at work, reading the newspapers to see if there had been any mention of any of the firm's clients or if there were any articles that might be of interest to Ivor's clients. 'Morning Juliette,' he grunted as he slid into his chair. 'Hello, Ivor,' she replied and continued perusing the columns of *The Times*. Ivor tried to clear his head and concentrate on the pile of post Juliette had heaped on his desk but his mind was still full of Harold Godfrey's erotic story. After a perfunctory ruffle through the mail he looked across at his attractive, immaculate secretary and fantasised about how she would look naked, writhing sensuously on the carpet as he made fast and furious love to her. With an effort he expunged the delicious picture from his brain and began to read a business letter from Sheena, his former secretary who he had made love to only two days before and who now worked for Bob Maxwell's show business empire.

He looked up again at Juliette who was sitting with her shapely mini-skirted legs provocatively crossed and her shorthand notebook and pen poised at the ready. 'Sheena's written to tell us that he'd like to see Ruff in the pages of a woman's magazine,' he informed her. 'But I think we need a fresh angle for the big weeklies to be interested.'

'How about offering an exclusive feature with colour photographs of the new house he's bought in Guildford?' Juliette suggested.

'Good thinking, but I've already sold the idea to the *Daily Mirror*. Anyhow, I don't think we'd better have too many in-depth photographs unless Ruff allows us to search through every room with a fine toothcomb beforehand,' said Ivor drily. He clasped is hands behind his head as he rocked to and fro in his executive chair, smiling as he recalled how, just minutes before a team from Granada TV had arrived to film an interview, Ruff's manager had narrowly averted disaster by hiding a pile of Scandinavian magazines with titles like *Sailor*, *Teenage Colts* and *Young Lions* he had spotted in Ruff's dressing room.

'Why? Is it true that he's a woofter?' asked Juliette carelessly.

Ivor looked at her sharply and chose his words with care. 'Ruff's sexual preferences are never, repeat, never to be discussed outside this office or even, come to think of it, with other people here who don't work on his publicity.'

Juliette shrugged her shoulders and said: 'It's no big deal as far as I'm concerned, but you should realise that lots of people are wondering whether Ruff's queer.'

'So long as they don't do more than wonder, otherwise he's finished! Personally I don't see why all those Mums and Dads who'd be so horrified to find out that Ruff's bent should be so up-tight about it. After all, if they thought the thing through, they'd see that all those sixteen-year-olds who throw their knickers on stage and try to waylay him in hotels are really quite safe.

'Mind you, these days, I doubt if half of those kids still have their cherries intact,' he added darkly.

'Oh, come on, Ivor, not all of us began screwing at twelve years old like you,' said Juliette with a saucy smile.

Her boss looked at her in astonishment. 'What makes you think I was such an early starter?' said Ivor mildly. 'If you really want to know, I didn't cross the Rubicon till I was seventeen.'

'Seventeen's just about the right age,' said Juliette thoughtfully. But before she could expand on this remark, the internal telephone buzzed and she picked up the receiver. 'There's a girl named Kirsty Moss from the Churchmill Agency to see you, Ivor, shall I bring her up?'

'Sure, no hold on a sec, bring her along to the boardroom instead, it's always free on Tuesday mornings – and would you mind making coffee after you've shown her in?'

Ivor gathered up a pad, pencil and folder and walked briskly up the stairs to the lushly appointed boardroom. He only had to wait a minute before Juliette opened the door to introduce the first model from Leon Standlake's agency who had come to audition for the Golden Tan

Capsules campaign and Ronnie Bloom's latest swimwear catalogue.

'Ivor, this is Kirsty,' announced Juliette and a tall, blonde girl swept into the room. He looked up and tried unsuccessfully to repress a startled stare at the dazzling blonde girl who now stood before him dressed in a tight, figure-hugging, baby-blue minidress which was tailored to make grown men cry, as Ivor was later to confide to Brian Lipman. She was of medium height with long golden hair which she wore simply down the sides of her high cheekbones. Her sparkling azure-blue eyes alone were enough to send Ivor's pulse racing, though his eyes travelled down her supple, slender body and his gaze swivelled to the swelling mounds of her beautifully formed breasts which jutted out like two firm fruits ripe for the mouth.

'Ivor Belling?' enquired this luscious girl, holding out her hand. 'I'm Kirsty Moss from the Churchmill Agency. Leon's told me about the work. I hope that I'm what you're looking for.'

'Good to meet you,' mumbled Ivor awkwardly, trying to regain his composure and prevent any further stirring in his groin. 'Yes, we're looking for two blonde girls as a matter of fact. Er, would you like some coffee whilst I look over your portfolio?'

'No thank you, not for me,' she said and not wishing to be further interrupted, Ivor turned to his secretary and said: 'I don't think I'll bother either, Juliette, and by the way, hold all my calls for now, please.'

He settled down and Kirsty passed him a loose-leaf photograph album. 'I'm surprised I haven't seen you before,' said Ivor. He opened the album and looked at a monochrome photograph of the model in a mink coat. She looked unbelievably sultry as she sat in the front passenger seat of a Cadillac limousine, with the door wide open and her long legs facing towards the camera as she sat poised to swing her feet down to the ground.

'I signed up with Leon Standlake last month,' she

explained, 'though I only started modelling last year when I was working in New York.'

Ivor looked up and said: 'How long were you in the States?'

'About six months. I went over as a mother's help but the husband of the family I worked for was in the rag trade and he fixed me up with an agency when things went a little haywire at home.'

Ivor smiled and said: 'Did the kids get on your nerves? Anyway, you're wasted as a mother's help. You look far too glamorous to be a nanny!'

'Oh, I love children, but there was an embarrassing incident concerning Ralph, the sixteen-year-old son of the house, which caused some trouble. His mother thought it best that I leave and take up another job.'

Kirsty paused and then said softly: 'Actually, Leon thought you might like to hear more about what happened. He also said that you were a nice guy who can be trusted to keep a secret.'

He pricked up his ears and leaned back in his comfortable executive chair. 'I'm flattered but sure, in this business, above all, you must learn to be discreet and respect a confidence.'

'Good enough, I'll tell you then. The simple fact was that Ralph had a crush on me from the minute I arrived. He was a nice boy, blond like me and good looking, too, though he wasn't big for is age. He was only fifteen when I arrived to help his mother look after his younger brother of seven and his sister aged five. If anything, Ralph looked even younger than his age and he was a quiet boy, very polite and helpful.

'Well, one weekend shortly after his sixteenth birthday, his parents went to stay overnight with some friends in Philadelphia and they took the two younger kids with them but left Ralph behind. He said he wanted to study for his school exams which were coming up soon. I usually had Sundays free but I said I didn't mind staying with Ralph and taking a day off during the week instead. But

123

on the Saturday afternoon Brian, his best friend, telephoned Ralph to invite him to a party at an older boy's house just over a mile away. I saw no reason to call his parents and ask them if Ralph could go as I knew they approved of his friendship with Brian, so I simply warned him not to come home too late. I had no plans to go out and I stayed in the house on Saturday night and watched television. This was just as well for, unfortunately, some stupid idiot had brought a bottle of whisky to the party. As you might guess, Ralph, who had never drunk spirits in his life, got absolutely pissed out of his mind and had to be delivered home by taxi.

'The other lad had paid the driver and he kindly helped me carry Ralph to his room, take off his coat and jacket, and lay him on the bed before he left. I decided that I'd better undress him, and I pulled off his shoes and socks. His shirt came off easily enough and I ran my hand along his smooth, hairless chest but he was now completely out for the count and didn't even wake up when I unbuckled his belt and unzipped his fly. I pulled down his trousers and hung them up with his other clothes in the wardrobe. Ralph moaned softly in his sleep and when I turned back to see if all was well with him, he was lying flat on his back. I couldn't help noticing a huge bulge in his underpants.'

She gave an awkward smile and Ivor cleared his throat. 'Well, I can't say I'm altogether surprised,' he commented. 'After all, he'd just turned sixteen so he'd reached puberty, hadn't he, and he must have been having an erotic dream.'

Kirsty nodded but held up her hand before Ivor could continue. 'Yes, of course, but honestly, it looked like he had a giant tent peg stuffed in his pants! Well, I have to admit it, Ivor, curiosity got the better of me and carefully I pulled down his pants. I looked down and saw this huge, young, fresh-as-the-driven-snow circumcised cock standing up smartly at attention from a crown of straggly blond pubic hair at its root. I couldn't help admiring the size of this lovely big prick which must have been at least eight or even nine inches long. It was at least as thick as my last boyfriend, who was more than adequately well-endowed. A tingling wave of passion swept over me (in my defence I hadn't made love since getting to America) but though I felt myself getting wet between my legs, I just threw a duvet over the boy and went to my bedroom to get undressed and go to bed myself.

'I had just taken off my knickers and was standing naked by my bed when I suddenly heard a groan coming from Ralph's bedroom. It flashed through my mind that he might be sick and I had best drag him to the bathroom as quickly as possible.

'So without even thinking about the fact that I was absolutely starkers, I rushed into his room but my young man was sleepwalking – or to be exact, sleepwanking! His eyes were tightly shut but his hand was grasped round his cock and he was tossing himself off at a great rate of knots. He heaved himself out of bed and staggered off in the direction of the toilet, frigging himself furiously. I waited for a moment and then followed him along the landing to the loo. The door was open and there was Ralph, sitting on the toilet with his head thrown back and resting on the cistern. His eyes were still closed and he was breathing heavily as he continued to rub his cock faster and faster. I stood by the open doorway, transfixed by the spectacle as Ralph reached his climax and the sperm shot out of his twitching tool and trickled over his fingers. With a sigh he got up and I stepped aside as he stepped towards the door. His now flaccid penis flapped between his thighs as he lurched back to his bedroom and I heard a gentle thud as he threw himself down on the bed. I tip-toed back along the landing and looked in but Ralph was still in a deep sleep but was now lying on his stomach, snoring slightly with a satisfied smile on his face.

'But perhaps it would be better to wake him up? No, best to leave him be, I thought, and remembering my Red Cross training, I crept up to the bed and moved his arms up and his head to one side to prevent him choking in case he vomited. Finally I turned off the light before shutting the door quietly behind me. I walked slowly back to my room and slipped between the sheets. A powerful wave of desire for Ralph's youthful body shuddered through me and I began to feel the familiar sensations flow out from my damp pussy. With a quickening pulse I ran my hand over my tingling nipples. They rose and hardened as I imagined Ralph's boyish fresh face pressed against them and his full, rich lips taking my erect red tits into his mouth. Then I thought about how his gorgeous young cock could slew a path through my love channel and how I could grip the rampant, throbbing shaft and direct the smooth rounded head inside my raging quim.

'I squeezed my titties with my fingers and my entire body tingled with erotic pleasure as I ran my hand down my tummy towards the tangled mass of hair at the base. Twining the silky strands around my fingers, I slipped a finger into the wet warmth of my honeypot. I raised my knees and when I found my clitty and began to massage it, I started to writhe with ecstacy on the now rumpled sheets and thrust two and then three fingers in and out of my sticky cunt. My bottom rubbed sensuously against the cool linen and very soon I brought myself off. My tangy love juice flooded out as my body relaxed, whilst I scolded myself for even thinking about making love to the sleeping sixteen-year-old youth in the next bedroom.

'It took me a little while to get to sleep but finally I dozed off. The next morning I peeped into Ralph's bedroom before I showered and dressed. He was still asleep but there was no reason to wake him so I made myself breakfast. I was reading the newspaper when I heard the first stirrings from his room. I trotted upstairs and knocked on his door. "Come in," he groaned and though Ralph looked a little tousled, he seemed to be okay except for a thumping headache. "That'll teach you to overindulge," I said, though not unkindly because we all seem to have to go through this rite of passage. "Do you remember how much you had to drink?"

'"Too much!" he muttered, holding his head in his hands. "In future I'll stick to cola."

'"Very wise," I said and I sat down on his bed and placed my palm against Ralph's forehead. "After all, what would have happened to you if your friends hadn't bundled you into a taxi and I hadn't been here to put you to bed."

'He looked at me sharply but said nothing as I advised: "An occasional drink won't do you any harm, but you must treat alcohol, and especially spirits, just like you would treat one of your girl-friends – with care and consideration!"

'And with those fine words I swept out of the room, leaving the poor lad to regret his folly. By lunchtime, though, he had fully recovered. We were sitting on stools at the kitchen bar eating roast beef sandwiches when Ralph suddenly blurted out: "Look, I want to apologise about last night, and I don't really want to talk about it any more, but there is something I'd like to ask you."

'"Of course you can, Ralph," I said encouragingly. He took a deep breath and his face coloured as he paused for a moment and then continued in a rush of words: "Kirsty, did you undress me after the taxi driver brought me home?"

'I looked at him straight in the eye and nodded and this made Ralph blush even deeper. "Then you saw me naked? Oh God!" he groaned but I hastened to assure him that he had nothing to be ashamed of. "Far from it," I added, putting my hand on his arm. "You're a very well made young man!" He smiled wryly and said with a note of bitterness in his voice: "Thanks for the compliment, Kirsty, though I'd give anything to know why I'm the only guy in the class who hasn't yet made a home run."

'I didn't understand what he meant at first but then I realised that the good-looking boy was still waiting for his first fuck. I had to bite my lip to stop myself telling Ralph that I would give anything to initiate him into the joys of sex! Instead, to try and cool his ardour, I suggested that we played a set or two of tennis as we had a court laid out at the bottom of the garden. He brightened up at the idea and I said: "I'm not very good but I'll give you a game if I can borrow a racket."

'"No problem, see you on court," he said and we went upstairs to change. Although I knew that my only tennis skirt was a mini which ended barely inches below my bum, perhaps it was an unconsciously powerful feeling of desire deep inside me which wanted to excite Ralph that made me pull on a pair of sheer, almost transparent tight white panties and put on a bra which lifted my breasts even higher. My heart leaped when I saw Ralph on the tennis court, he looked so pretty in his dinky white tennis shorts that I could have ravished him then and there.

'Well, we played tennis for about an hour and then, with a spontaneity I hadn't experienced for a long time, I let my secret feelings get the better of me. It happened whilst we were walking back to the house for a cold drink, Ralph stopped and bent down to tie up a flapping shoelace. I leaned back against the trunk of a small tree, with one foot raised on a toybox for the younger children which was kept outside in the garden during the summer. Deliberately, I opened my legs wide so that the sun shone on my crotch. From his kneeling position Ralph could see my panties and make out the outline of my cunt in the glistening afternoon light.

'I closed my eyes, allowing the warmth of the sun to seep through me. It filled me with an acute sense of awareness of my physical needs. Ralph said nothing as I moved my hand across and ruffled the curly blond hair of his head, though I could hear his breathing quicken as my fingers lazily traced their way down to his neck. He stood up and leaned his face towards me and it seemed like the most natural thing in the world to give his cheek a little kiss, though I did let my lips linger whilst my hip rubbed against his groin. Ralph grabbed me and kissed me full on the mouth. His teeth nipped at my lower lip as I reeled into his arms and he hugged me. We sank down on a hummock of earth and I discovered that, though he might have never made a home run, he had long passed first base because he certainly knew how to kiss. His tongue curled around mine, around and around and then it waggled around in my mouth as his hands roved all over my breasts.

'I broke away from the embrace and whispered: "Not here, Ralph, not here, we'll get all dirty. Come on, let's go back inside the house." Well now, I don't know who was the most eager but we ran back indoors in record time, hand in hand, and we resumed our amorous clinch upstairs in my bedroom. He was trembling with youthful lust but I made him follow my example and take off his shoes and socks before lying down with me on my bed. In a trice his hands were under my shirt and despite his obvious inexperience he managed to unhook my bra without too much difficulty before he lifted the cups and put his shaking hands on my tingling titties. By this time I was feeling so sexy that I made a grab for his lap to take hold of that thrillingly big cock which I had seen him play with the night before. But, to my disappointment, all I could just feel there was a soft tube of flesh between his upper thighs.

'However, I was now fully aroused and I unhooked my skirt and let it fall to the ground. Then I tugged my shirt over my head and my bra fell off at the same time so I was now nude except for my moistening panties. His fingertips brushed against my breasts and my nipples immediately jumped up to attention. "Do you like my titties, Ralph? Why don't you suck them for me, there's a good boy."

'He hesitated for a minute and I realised that he had never reached this stage before with a girl. So gently, I pulled his face down between the valley of my white, rounded globes. I pushed my breasts together as his lips caressed the soft flesh. Ralph was a quick learner for he licked and lapped vigorously at my engorged red titties, his tongue constantly moving which sent wild vibrations throughout my body. I was so carried away by now that I peeled off my panties and guided his hand down over my tummy to my pussy, clamping my thighs round his hand as his fingers caressed my hairy bush.

'My cunny fairly throbbed, my sticky juices now running over Ralph's fingers and his tongue slid wickedly round my nipples. His hand now moved in and out of my sopping cunt. My back arched in ecstasy as his skilful fingers slithered over my clitty, sending me into deliriums of pure joy. Now was the time to reciprocate and I moved my hands across his slender, boyish hips and tugged down his shorts and pants. He took his hand out of my love-box to pull his singlet over his head, but his bare cock was not yet fully stiff, though it still looked thick and meaty enough. I took it in my fist and rubbed my hand up and down the hot, velvet pole. But still his prick would not harden and Ralph almost cried with fruitless rage as his hand left my pussy to join mine in mauling, pressing and squeezing his recalcitrant penis.

'"You're just nervous," I assured him. "Don't worry, there's another way to get it up which almost always works. Just lie back and relax and leave everything to me." I'm not sure if he knew what I meant but nevertheless he did as he was told and after kissing his face my head moved swiftly down to his stubborn prick. I brought my lips across the smooth rounded knob. I let my tongue run the full length of the shaft down to the hairs around the root before running my lips back to the top. I gave it a quick little moistening lick before taking the purple helmet into my mouth.'

She paused dramatically and Ivor wiped the sheen of perspiration which had formed on his brow as he crossed his legs to hide the growing bulge which had appeared in the front of his trousers. 'Did this do the trick?' he croaked in a hoarse voice and Kirsty nodded brightly. 'It worked like a charm,' she said happily. 'As soon as I started sucking, his cock swelled up to its fullest dimensions and young Ralph was in the seventh heaven of delight as my lips worked up and down his jerking tool. I only had time to gobble it in one more time before he spunked inside my mouth. I sucked and swallowed every last drop of his gushy cream until his prick stopped twitching and began shrinking back to its normal size.

'But at that age, of course, most boys are able to continue almost immediately. Now that Ralph's initial nervousness had worn off, it only took a minute or so before I had rubbed his shaft up to another marvellous thick, stiff erection. It was wicked, I know, but Ivor, I just had to have that gorgeous young cock inside me!

'So I raised my head slowly and keeping my fingers wrapped round his pulsating pole I said rather pompously: "Now Ralph, this is the moment of truth. Are you sure you are ready to cross the bridge into manhood?" It was an unnecessary question as the hardness of his cock as it quivered in my hand was answer enough. Instinctively he rolled on top of me and I spread my legs as wide as possible, keeping my hand on his throbbing cock. I guided his knob through the slippery entrance of my cunny lips and he trembled all over, overcome with emotion of the moment. His shaft squelched its way into a warm, wet cunt for the very first time.

'Ralph lay motionless and I opened my eyes and looked up at him. "Very good, Ralph darling. Now be a good boy and fuck me."

'"I'm not too sure exactly what I should do," he confessed anxiously.

'I couldn't help smiling as I said: "It's very easy – just pull your lovely cock out of my cunt and then push it back in until you feel the spunk rushing through your shaft. Then you just let nature take its course. Don't worry, I'm on the pill so you don't have to worry about coming inside me." My hands slipped down to clasp the cheeks of his taut, firm bottom and young Ralph proved himself to be a quick learner. His arms went under my shoulders as I eagerly lifted my hips to welcome his thrusting, virile young cock which now slid beautifully inside my juicy cunt.

'What he lacked in experience he certainly made up for in enthusiasm, bouncing up and down on top of me as I clawed his jerking bum to pull him even further inside my squelchy love channel. His pumping became even more frenzied as he plunged his prick deeper and deeper. He rode me as wildly as a jockey in sight of the finishing post and not surprisingly, before I had a chance to come with him, he spurted his spunk. After a few further frantic quiverings, his shaft began to droop and he took it out of me and rolled over on his back, gasping for breath. Not as satisfying as it could have been for me, but understandable in the circumstances.'

'Yes, he was drained emotionally and physically from the experience,' agreed Ivor, nodding his head. 'I remember my own first attempt at love-making. I couldn't wait to finish so that I could say to myself I'd actually done it at last!'

Kirsty licked her lips and murmured: 'I'm sure you've gained a lot more experience since then.' She looked sensuously at Ivor who smiled and said: 'Not as much as you'd think and I'm always ready to learn.' Their eyes locked and there was a sensual silence in the room which Kirsty broke as she cleared her throat and said: 'I hope I'll be able to tell you what happened afterwards but I'm afraid I've already taken up too much of your time.'

Ivor glanced at his watch. 'Yes, I have quite a busy schedule today but let me look through your photographs. You're twenty-two, aren't you? I think I might go for a younger girl for our Golden Tan promotion but your figure looks fine for the swimwear catalogue we have to start work on early next week. Would you be interested in that?'

'Oh yes, thank you very much. I'm free until Friday week.'

'Okay then, if you work as well as you tell an arousing tale, then we'll have no problems,' he grinned – and a saucy smile spread across Kirsty's face too.

'It was all true, I promise you! With most men I

wouldn't have gone into such great detail, but Leon Standlake assured me that you're very much a man of the world. And from that bulge sticking up in your lap, I can see you enjoyed listening to my little memoir.'

'Well, I do like to hear a good sexy story,' confessed Ivor, who made no move to stop Kirsty from sitting down on his thigh and stroking his stiff prick which stood up so prominently between his legs. My God, he thought, many model girls were randy but this girl was something else, as she slipped off his thighs and knelt between his legs. She unzipped his trousers and eased them down over his knees together with his underpants, leaving his bare cock to stand up rigidly. She stroked it gently along its length as she cradled his balls.

Ivor groaned and writhed as the girl went down on him, juicing his knob with her saliva as she forced his knob between her lips. He let his hands play with her hair and lay back as she gobbled furiously on his throbbing shaft. Then she eased back, licking along the underside of his cock until she reached his balls which she sucked into her mouth and swished around before licking up to the helmet, taking the shaft now in a wonderful deep-throating action until Ivor could feel her nose nuzzling his crinkly public hair.

Ivor came quickly, exploding in hot jets which filled her mouth though Kirsty continued sucking, milking his prick to the last drop until she felt it begin to soften. 'M'mm, quite delicious! I don't have lunch, as I'm on a strict diet, but I hope you'll be able to be at the shoot around the mid-morning break.'

'I'll certainly try,' promised Ivor, hastily pulling up his trousers.

'Do you know that there are some girls who don't indulge in fellatio. But I love sucking cocks, though most men can't wait to climax! It's so exciting when the jism spurts out! Nothing tastes so tangy and clean as spunk and it's nutritious too, full of minerals like potassium and zinc as well as vitamin C.'

There was a knock on the door and Juliette came in. 'There's another girl from the Churchmill Agency to see you, Ivor. Her name's Penny Williams. Shall I bring her up?'

'Oh, she's a lovely girl,' exclaimed Kirsty, gathering up her folder of photographs and handbag. 'She's a wild, dark skinned girl with a gorgeous tan. She's just come back from a glamour shoot in Lanzarote. We've never worked together so I hope you like her.'

'I'll look at her photographs carefully,' he said, lightly squeezing her proferred hand. 'Juliette will show you down. Thanks for coming, Kirsty, see you next week.'

Ivor chose Penny Williams to be Kirsty's partner for the swimwear catalogue but by lunchtime he still had not found a suitable girl to head the Golden Tan promotion. He decided to take a quick lunch at Yummies. Perhaps Samantha, who he had first met there, would also be having one of Geraldine's generous smoked salmon and salad platters or hot salt beef sandwiches on rye bread. Sam would be ideal for the job, with her light complexion and flowing blonde hair, he thought. 'But I don't think she'd abandon her legal studies,' he said aloud as he pushed open the door of the sandwich bar and joined the short queue waiting to be served.

'It's the first sign of madness, Ivor,' said a jolly voice. He whirled round to see the grinning figure of Brian Lipman standing behind him.

'Talking to yourself,' added the photogapher patiently. 'That's the first sign of madness, and the only known cure is to buy lunch today for the best photogapher in London.'

Ivor sighed and clapped his old friend on the shoulder. 'Don't I know it,' he said sadly. 'And isn't it my bad luck that David Bailey's out of town today and Martin Reece has my table in the River Room at the Savoy all this week.'

'Never mind, the cure's also effective if the photographer's initials are BL and you buy him a round of salt beef on rye with new green cucumbers and a portion of *lutkas*,' insisted Brian Lipman. 'Tell you what, I'll buy the cokes and meet you at the table.'

As they munched through their sandwiches, Lipman asked Ivor if he had chosen the models for the new swimsuit catalogue. 'I've hired two of Leon Standlake's girls, Kirsty Moss and Penny Williams. Have you worked with either of them before?'

'I've not heard of Penny Williams but I know Kirsty, she's a strange one, that girl. I'll lay odds she gave you a blow job at the audition.'

Ivor stared at him. 'How the hell did you know?' he asked, feeling a trifle miffed at the idea that Kirsty was known for the sweet suction of her lips rather than her abilities in front of the camera.

The photographer threw out his arms. 'It's her speciality, Ivor, and believe me, she's done very well out of it. Don't worry though, Kirsty's marvellous in front of the cameras.'

But Ivor was still unhappy with himself. 'I was very unprofessional,' he scowled. 'I shouldn't have been swayed by anything but her suitability for the job. Instead, I'd already made up my mind to give Kirsty the job even before I'd even studied her portfolio.'

'Don't be too hard on yourself,' advised Lipman after calling out to Geraldine for two pieces of apple strudel. 'I hear she walked away with the Nayland Holidays calendar job from Shackletons after Terry Cooney had interviewed her – and between you and me I've also engaged Kirsty after having the treatment. Listen, she doesn't put herself out for every Tom, Dick and Harry, only for the blokes she takes a shine to.

'Anyway, I happen to know that she's living with a very strange fellow who likes hearing about what she does when she goes to auditions. He gets a kick out of listening to her describe how she sucks off all these guys, just as some men get their rocks off by looking on whilst their wives screw their mates.'

He could see a look of disbelief on Ivor's face and he

continued: 'What, you don't think that happens? Let me tell you something, I found myself involved in what could have been a very embarrassing situation indeed last week. I'm doing some photos for the jackets of a new paperback series and last week I set up the props in the studio for a bedroom scene. Actually it was for a novel by your old mate Mike McGribble, who was at college with you.'

'Mike McGribble? I thought he went to work for one of those big foods company after he left university.'

'He might have done but he now writes full-time and does bloody well, I can tell you. He doesn't write under his own name, of course, but I'll bet you've picked up an Ed Bell paperback at the station or airport.'

'Mike's Ed Bell? The guy that writes those racy stories? Everyone tut-tuts about them but they still buy thousands of them every time a new one comes out.' Ivor gawped in utter astonishment. 'Christ, I never knew that, though I haven't seen him for years. Of course, I can see why his publishers thought he needed a pseudonym, McGribble isn't a great come-on monicker, is it? So did he come along to the studio and see the photographs being taken?'

'No, authors don't often get involved in the design of their book jackets. The publishers just sent me a sketch of what they wanted, so I set up a big double bed in the studio. I engaged a young couple called Marion and Pete, who are actually husband and wife in real life. I also booked a nice young chap called Tommy Biggs who you might have seen on TV picking up the girl and carrying her off to the forest in that new toothpaste commercial.

'Well, the book's about a young couple who weren't hitting it off between the sheets. The scene I had to shoot was when the husband catches his wife in bed with her boy friend whilst they were on holiday in Bournemouth. I thought Pete would want to play the boy friend so that he'd be in bed with Marion but he said he'd prefer to be the husband who stands in the doorway in swimming trunks and with a towel round his neck as if he's just come up from the hotel swimming pool. It didn't really matter one

136

way or the other to me so I agreed and we started work. Marion and Pete went into the changing room to get ready and I suggested that Tom changed on set and spread his clothes out around the place to give the shot an authentic look. So he stripped down to his pants and lay on the bed whilst I arranged his clothes on the eiderdown. Marion came back wearing only a long, baggy tee shirt which only partially concealed the fact that, according to her agency card, her figure measurements were a lush 38–24–34. Pete wore a pair of very brief cream trunks which bulged so impressively that I wondered if he'd just been giving his wife a quick grope behind the curtains.

'Anyhow, Martion lifted up her tee shirt and bared her enormous pair of provocatively ripe breasts. She had taken off her panties so her thick, brown bush of pubic hair was also revealed. She jumped onto the bed and said carelessly: "How would you like me, Brian? Lying on my tummy and wiggling my bum or sitting up with my arms around Tommy?"

'"I think we'll start with you both sitting up together with your arms wrapped round each other," I said and she snuggled close up to Tommy, who looked a little bit unsure. "Go on, get really close, Tommy, you've just made passionate love to this gorgeous girl. I want you looking absolutely relaxed so you'll have a look of great shock on your face when the unsuspecting husband suddenly opens the door. Come on, let's try it, one, two, three, go!"

'But poor Tommy just couldn't get into the swing of things – he looked far too wooden. I was about to suggest that he changed places with Pete when Marion said to me with a wink: "I think I know how to get him going, Brian." She pulled back the eiderdown and before he could even say a word of protest, she tugged down Tommy's pants and exposed his floppy shaft which dangled down limply over his balls. "No wonder we're not getting anywhere, Tommy, you've got to put your heart and soul into a performance," she scolded him, tapping his prick with her finger. "Let's see if we can get you in the mood." She licked her lips and then bent over and held his bare cock in her hands, rubbing her fist up and down the shaft until it began to swell and harden as she wrapped her lips around his knob. I tell you, Ivor, the sight of her little pink tongue slithering around his shaft turned me on as much as Tommy!

'Marion sucked his tool until she felt he was about to blast off and then she lifted her head and continued to jerk him off as she placed his hand around one of her gorgeous tits. Her hand pounded hard and fast up and down his shaft and in a few seconds he jetted his jism all over her hand, though she didn't let go till he had spurted the last sticky drains of spunk.

'"There, that'll relax you," she said briskly. I looked round to where her husband Pete was standing at the door. Oh Christ, he'll go barmy, I thought, but how wrong I was – he wasn't frothing at the mouth with anger but was simply standing there with a look of ecstacy on his face, his swimming costume on the ground. It was obvious that he'd been tossing himself off watching his wife masturbate Tommy's tool. It did the trick, though, and I got the picture I wanted. Then Marion said: "Come on, Brian, join in the fun. Wouldn't you like to come over here and suck my titties?"

'Wouldn't I just! As Tommy rolled off the bed I padded across and cuddled her generous, curvey body. I licked her big nipples up to erection and she pulled off my trousers. My stiffie stood proudly waiting as she gave a big smile and then wriggled across to push her mouth over my throbbing cock. Then she muttered: "Quick, now fuck me hard!" and she lay back and opened her legs. I hesitated at first but Pete, who was standing at the foot of the bed, encouraged me to comply. "Go on, be a sport! Marion needs a good going-over, don't you, darling?" For answer she grabbed hold of my prick and guided it right up her hot, juicy cunt. I flexed myself and began ramming home. She circled my waist with her legs, bucking to and fro with her buttocks, lifting herself off the bed as I pumped away. She screamed out as I brought her off and she squeezed my balls as I shot my load inside her sopping honeypot.'

'And Marion's husband didn't mind?' Ivor marvelled. 'What did he do afterwards, make you a cup of tea?'

'No, not quite. I thought, while she's in the mood, I'll take some photos for my American contacts. So I heaved myself off and said to Pete: "Let me get back behind the camera. You do the rest." He was now more than ready so Marion sat astride him and lowered her dripping crack on his stiff cock. She thrust herself up and down on Pete's prick and as she raised herself up I got a perfect shot of the purple helmet of his penis, gleaming wet with her cunny juices, half-buried between her dribbling pussy lips. I managed to take about eight or nine good fuck shots which should bring in at least a couple of hundred dollars. My agent keeps the loot there for me so when I go to New York this summer I'll have a nice little bankroll waiting for me.'

'Good for you,' murmured Ivor. Suddenly his heart missed a beat. He looked up to see Samantha Garrett come into the sandwich bar. 'Brian, would you excuse me a minute?' he said. 'There's a girl just come in who I must speak to.'

He waited till she was served and then just as she was leaving he placed his hand on her shoulder. 'Hi, Sam, how are you?' he said quietly.

'Hello Ivor, not so bad. Are you keeping busy?' she replied. She was about to leave when Ivor gently pulled her arm. 'I've got a table over here. Won't you stay and have your lunch with me?' The lovely blonde girl hesitated and said in a low voice. 'I thought we'd agreed to cool things for a couple of weeks.'

'Oh come on, Sam,' urged Ivory persuasively. 'I didn't know you were going to have lunch at Yummies, did I? Can't we even have a coffee together until you decide if you want to go out with me?'

After a brief pause she gave a small smile and nodded her head. 'Of course we can, Ivor, sorry, I'm being silly,' she said and followed him back to the table where Brian Lipman stood up. 'Brian, meet Samantha Garrett. Sam, this is Brian Lipman, he's a photographer who does a lot of work for our agency.'

'Nice to meet you, Sam, but I'm afraid I have to shoot off. They're hard taskmasters at Cable Publicity, you see, and they pay so little I can only afford lunch three times a week,' said the photographer, offering Sam his chair. 'No, really, I must dash. Thanks for the sandwich, Ivor, my turn to pay next year.'

They made small talk whilst Sam finished her sandwich and then Ivor went to the bar and brought over two coffees. 'Sam, there's a smashing film on at the Plaza tonight, the new Pink Panther movie, *A Shot In The Dark*. Why don't we go and see it? Peter Sellers is always good for a laugh. We could have a quick bite first.' She looked at him with a pained annoyance.

'Ivor, I wish you wouldn't press me,' she said softly as she looked steadily at him. 'We had an agreement, remember?'

'I know we did, Sam,' he confessed. 'But honestly, I would so love to see you again. Please say yes.' She said nothing and, as Ivor sensed he was winning the argument, he pressed on: 'I don't know about you, but I need cheering up to face this afternoon. I've two dreary reports to write and I'll do them much better knowing I have something nice to look forward to this evening.'

Sam wriggled her shoulders and said reluctantly: 'An agreement is an agreement, Ivor, and they aren't meant to be broken.'

'Maybe so, but wasn't it Sam Goldwyn who said something about a verbal agreement not being worth the paper it's signed on!'

This made Sam smile and she finally nodded her head and said: 'Well, alright, Ivor, but it's strictly a one-off, alright? Can you pick me up from work at half past six? I have to stay late for a client conference but I'll be ready by then.'

'No problem, Sam,' he said happily. 'Then we can then go straight to Luigi's in Charlotte Street for a plate of pasta. It must have been fate us meeting like this, you know, because I brought my car in today and I've parked very near your office.'

'Go on, off you go, I'll see you late,' she said and Ivor kissed her cheek as he rose from the seat.

The afternoon dragged on but Ivor managed to finish both reports well before he had to leave. He passed his hand over his face and decided to borrow Martin Reece's electric razor which the managing director kept in his office. Cable Publicity officially closed at half past five and after he said goodbye to Juliette he made his way to Martin's office.

Earlier in the afternoon Martin had informed him that he was going out to Luton to see a possible new client and wouldn't return till the morning. Ivor didn't bother to knock but simply opened the door of Martin's office. He strode across to the shelf where he knew Martin kept his razor when he heard a voice come from behind the door which led to the boss's private bathroom.

'Come on Martin, come out of the shower and I'll dry you with this nice big bath towel,' trilled a familiar voice which Ivor recognised as belonging to Alex Lyttelton, a bouncy, vivacious secretary who had been working for the finance director, Clive Sawyer, for the past three months. With a grin, Ivor opened the door to see Martin's silhouette behind the frosted glass of the shower. Alex was wearing one of Ronnie Bloom's skimpy bikinis which left her creamy breasts almost totally exposed except for the nipples which were themselves barely covered by the tiny top.

As if she decided it was hardly worth wearing, Alex unhooked the flimsy top and let it flutter to the ground. She then pulled down the bottom half of the bikini and her pert little naked backside was stuck out towards Ivor as she called out again: 'Aren't you ready yet?' This time Martin appeared, shaking the moisture from his body as he walked towards the waiting girl. She wrapped him in the huge bath sheet and proceeded to dry him, taking especial care, it seemed to Ivor, of Martin's cock and balls. But when she removed the towel, his boss's prick was still dangling limply between his legs.

'Oh my, we can't have your little soldier standing at ease. I want him standing to attention,' cried Alex, opening a bottle of baby oil and tipping the soft liquid into her hand.

'Your wish is my command,' said Martin gallantly and sure enough his penis started to swell and harden as Alex gently slid one hand up and down his shaft and squeezed his hairy ballsack with the other. 'Is that nice?' she said rather unnecessarily – Martin's cock was now as stiff as a poker. Nevertheless, he nodded his head and she then added in a throaty voice: 'Well, if you like that, how about this?' She dropped to her knees in front of him and, taking his throbbing barrel-like penis in both hands, she began to swirl her tongue around his purple domed knob.

'A-a-a-h! That's wonderful, absolutely super,' crooned Martin, jerking his hips to and fro as he fucked her mouth slowly but firmly in long, smooth strokes.

Alex moved her mouth away and spread the towel out on the floor. She lay down upon it, resting her head on a heaped pile of towels. Martin knelt before her, his twitching tool raised high almost against his belly and she widened her legs in anticipation, drawing her knees up to allow an easy access to her love-box. I don't think I'd better interrupt them, thought Ivor, as he watched Martin press himself down, one hand squeezing Alex's large breast, his thumb flicking wildly against the rosy red stem of her nipple, and with the other hand cupping her rounded arse, levering her slightly upwards to bring his prick into perfect alignment with her pouting pussy lips. The randy pair moaned with delight as the moist grooves of Alex's excited cunny fitted lovingly around Martin's

142

sensitive helmet, sucking in his cock with lips that were even softer and sexier than Alex's mouth.

Martin savoured the blissful few seconds of an impending bout of love-making before tensing his hips and driving his tool deep into Alex's cunt. Her thighs wobbled as she received the last few inches of Martin's sizeable shaft inside her. He stayed still for a moment and then started to slide his prick in and out of her tingling pussy. Soon she clamped her legs round Martin's waist and cried out: 'Come on, big boy! Fuck me till my cunney's full of your sticky hot spunk!'

She pulled Martin's buttocks towards her, slapping them in rhythm to his powerful humping and before long she screamed out: 'Yes! Yes! Yes!' and she rolled around, working her cunt back and forth against the ramming of Martin's thick prick. He shuddered with pleasure as he sheathed his pulsating shaft so fully inside her cunt that his balls nestled against her arsehole. Then faster and faster he slid his tool backwards and forwards until, with a hoarse groan, his prick began to tremble. Thick squirts of sperm shot out from the 'eye' of his knob. Alex squealed in delight as she milked his cock dry and Martin collapsed, limp and exhausted on top of her.

Ivor closed the door silently and resisted the temptation to caress his own erection which protruded out from his crotch. He stood still when he heard Martin say: 'What was that? Is somebody there?' and smiled when Alex replied: 'No-one's here, they all think you've gone to Luton, you clever boy. I only wish my parents would go out one night and we could make love in comfort in my bed and not worry about someone catching us out.'

Don't worry, your secret's safe with me, said Ivor to himself as he tip-toed across Martin's office and reached out for the electric razor which Martin kept on top of a pile of trade magazines. Mind, whilst Martin was entitled to do as he pleased, if he made a habit of screwing a secretary instead of keeping an appointment to see a possible new client, the agency would soon find itself up the proverbial creek. It wasn't like Martin to play around with the staff, mused Ivor, as he plugged in the razor in the downstairs men's room. The founder and managing director of the old firm always insisted that mixing business and pleasure that way could lead to dangerous consequences. For instance, a discarded mistress who worked for Cable Publicity might take it into her head to spill some confidential beans to a rival agency. Ivor resolved to have a discreet word with Martin about what he had seen.

He met Sam promptly at half past six and they shared a delicious huge bowl of spaghetti bolognese at Luigi's Trattoria before they walked to the car and Ivor drove to Piccadilly. The wheel of fortune was still swinging Ivor's way as he swept into a parking space only twenty yards away from the cinema. They both enjoyed the wild slapstick gags in *A Shot In The Dark* but, like most sequels, it was slightly disappointing. As Ivor remarked as he climbed into his car: 'Peter Sellers is a marvellous clown but the second bite of the cherry is never as good as the first, is it?'

'No, you can't duplicate the element of surprise,' agreed Sam. 'Still, it cheered me up, which was more than I can say for that weird film *Repulsion* I saw last week.'

'Is that the one with Catherine Deneuve? She's a real creamer,' said Ivor. 'She's one of the sexiest ladies on screen as far as I'm concerned.'

Sam rolled her eyes upwards and drummed her fingers on his thigh. 'Trust you to seek out the lowest common denominator,' she said with a chuckle. 'I'll save you the trouble of going to leer at her, though, as you won't like *Repulsion*. She plays a demented, frightened Belgian girl living in London. She kills her boy friend and her landlord when they try to help her because she's terrified of everything, especially sex.'

'Thanks, when I need to be depressed I'll go and see it,' said Ivor, and he cut across an oncoming cab as he swung back sharply into Piccadilly, which brought forth a rich response about his parentage from an outraged taxi driver.

'Steady, Ivor, I'd rather arrive alive,' said Sam mildly but Ivor growled and said: 'You have to do as you'll always get done by in London traffic, Sam. All that taxi had to do was slow down a fraction and let us in, but he couldn't bear the thought of letting someone go in front of him. It's only in London where the rule is, you're first – after me!'

But he took Sam's hint and drove more courteously back to her flat, even flashing his lights to signal his assent to a surprised bus driver who had been waiting in vain for someone to stop and let him lumber across the busy Edgware Road.

He slowed smoothly to a stop outside Sam's flat and she looked at him with an amused twinkle in her eye. 'Now suppose I said, good night, Ivor? It's rather late, so I won't ask you in for coffee as I have to be up early for work tomorrow morning. But thanks for the lovely evening and call me next week just as we agreed on Saturday night. What would you say to that?'

Ivor looked at her sorrowfully. 'I'd say, well at least let me walk you to the front door where I'd kiss you goodnight and go straight home.'

'You wouldn't try to make me change my mind?' she teased.

'I don't think I'd be able to convince you,' he sighed and then quickly added: 'Mind, when I got home I'd phone you and say goodbye again.'

'Why would you want to say goodbye again?'

'Before I put on the gas and put my head in the oven!' he murmured and Sam burst out laughing. 'You rotten so and so, that's emotional blackmail,' she complained, but she let herself be taken into his arms and cuddled. 'Okay, come in for a bit but honestly, Ivor, we both have work tomorrow so you can't stay too late.'

'I'll go quietly, govnor,' promised Ivor as he leaped out of the car and rushed round to open the passenger door.

Sam opened the front door of the large Victorian house. Inside the hall Sam fumbled in her handbag for the key of their first floor flat when a familiar groaning sound came from behind the door of the ground-floor apartment.

'Don't worry, it's only Maggie the Moaner and her boy friend screwing themselves silly,' said Sam briskly. 'Kate and I call her Maggie the Moaner – she's one of those people who think you have to scream and shout to enjoy sex. But she's a nice enough girl, even though she does drive us crackers when she brings back a boy friend to stay the night.'

'I blame the movies myself, they give the impression that you have to give an Oscar-winning performance every time you're in the sack,' remarked Ivor as they climbed the stairs. Sam found the key and they went inside to a darkened flat. 'That's funny, Katie doesn't usually go to bed till midnight and I knew she wasn't planning to go out tonight,' said Sam as she switched on the lights.

'Make yourself comfortable whilst I see if Katie's in or if she's gone out and left me a note,' said Sam, walking across to her flatmate's room. Ivor took off his coat and his jacket and sat patiently as he listened to a low murmur of voices coming from Katie's bedroom. Sam returned a couple of minutes later clutching a letter in her hand and a sad look on her pretty face. 'Poor Katie, she's feeling very low and went to bed early,' she explained. 'Do you remember my telling you how we became involved with those two American chaps, Louis and David?' Ivor held up his hand. 'Don't tell me, she's had a *Dear John* or I should say a *Dear Katie* brush-off letter from her guy, what was his name again?'

'David Nash, and yes, you're spot-on, he's sent a long letter to her saying that he thought it would be best if they stopped writing to each other. He's met a girl in Manhattan and they're living together in her flat. It wouldn't be right, he feels, for them to keep sending sexy letters to one another. I don't suppose one can really blame him.'

146

'Not really, Sam, after all, how would you feel if we were living together and I kept getting hot letters from another girl?'

She considered the matter and gave a little shrug. 'Yes, you're right of course, but that's not much comfort as far as Katie is concerned. Look, this is the previous letter David sent her. Katie guessed he was keen on this girl Tessa from the way he enthused about her. Would you like to read it whilst I put the kettle on and change into something more comfortable? Katie would like to know if you think it's genuine or if David's simply making up a story to make breaking up easier.'

'Let's have a peep,' said Ivor, taking the letter and settling down to peruse it. 'Oh, tea for me, Sam, if it isn't too much trouble.'

'No problem,' she called out and Ivor began to read, skipping over the introductory hope-you're-keeping-well paragraphs until he came to the heart of the epistle.

'Now I must tell you about a very wonderful experience which happened to me two days ago. You may remember I've written to you before about my cousin Patrick, who is the managing director of a small publishing house here in New York. Well, he and his wife invited me to a grand dinner party at his home on Long Island to honour one of their newest authors, a girl named Elaine Towell who has written a novel called "Locked Into Midnight" which Patrick expects to be a blockbuster when he publishes it later this year. He sent me a sample chapter and it's racy, pacey story, quite similar to Harold Robbins but with more rounded characters and written in a softer, deeper writing style.

Katie, I won't deceive you, Elaine and I just slotted together like pieces from a jigsaw. Elaine is an extraordinarily lovely girl with a golden halo of hair, blue eyes and a slender, supple figure. She was wearing a striking dress that left her shoulders bare and was held in place by a ruffle. I could hardly take my eyes off her throughout the meal where I was lucky enough to be placed on her right hand side. As we talked I had an overwhelming temptation to push the fragile dress down and bare the creamy breasts which were hidden in the glistening blue satin material. We talked together afterwards in the lounge and my heart leapt when she accepted my offer to drive her back to her apartment in Brooklyn.

She invited me in for a nightcap and, whilst we were sitting together on her sofa, I asked how it felt to have written a novel and have a publisher be so keen as my cousin. "Patrick always tells me how difficult it is to have a first novel published. It must be a wonderful experience," I said.

"Most first experiences are often the best," she replied quietly and she raised her face eagerly to mine, closing her eyes in readiness. The kiss came, softly at first, followed by a series of quick, flickering kisses as I covered her face, eyelids, her forehead, her cheeks and back to her lips which I crushed against mine.

I heard her sigh and felt her body tremble as my hand slipped behind her back and unzipped her dress. The dress fell away from her and she wriggled out of it, tugging down the satin sheath until she wriggled free and stepped out of it. She wore only brief lace panties and a brassiere which she unhooked herself, and I thrilled at the sight of her enchanting naked breasts, each topped by an engorged uptilted strawberry nipple, provocatively pointing upwards so tantalisingly close to my yearning mouth. Now she tugged down her panties and my eyes roved over her luscious curving hips and the golden triangle of fluffy golden pubic hair into which I ached to bury my rock-hard cock.

Elaine opened her arms and I moved towards her. As we hugged she began to plant small, passionate kisses on my lips and cheeks. She tugged at my tie to loosen it and with her long, slender fingers she unbuttoned the first three buttons on my shirt and kissed the dark hairs at the top of my chest. My prick was now threatening to burst of out my trousers and I unclipped my belt whilst Elaine unzipped my fly and brought out my stiff, throbbing penis. She squeezed it tenderly as I stroked her inner thighs, my fingers inching their way slowly up the smooth bare flesh to her pubic mound.

"David, do you want to make love to me?" she whispered. I could have sworn the most solemn oath as to the truthfulness of my reply when with the utmost sincerity I answered huskily: "More than anything else in this crazy world, Elaine."

"You really mean that, don't you?" she said, her crystal blue eyes shining as she scanned my face. "You aren't just saying that because you want an easy fuck?"

I slowly nodded my head and I stroked her shoulders and arms as she helped me finish undressing. I picked her up and carried her into the bedroom and I placed her tenderly on the sheets. My arms, strong and hard, were tight about her and as my hands parted her thighs I kissed those divine, rounded breasts, lapping the hard, bullet-like nipples as my fingers sought the curling blonde hair. I heard her moan with welcoming pleasure and my entire body shook as I ran my fingertips along her wet, open slit.

Now she took hold of my pulsing hard-on and placed the tip of my prick against her pouting pussy lips. Slowly, I entered her and we moved together in unison, Elaine's hips jerking upward to meet the fierce rhythm of my savage lunges as my penis cleaved through the clinging, moist tunnel of her cunt. We came together wildly, embracing, caressing, clutching each other with our hearts pounding and limbs flailing as together we rode the wind . . .

I moved into Elaine's apartment last week and I think it

*best if we now close our correspondence. Katie, I wish you
every happiness for the future and I know that one day you
will find the person with whom you want to spend the rest of
your life. As I have done.
Give my kindest regards to Samantha,
Yours ever,
David.*

'No doubt about this letter being written from the
heart,' commented Ivor, passing it back to Sam. She had
placed his mug of tea on a side table and was now sitting
beside him. 'I think Katie's best advised to clear David
Nash from her mind.'

'That's easier said than done, Ivor. She's very cut up
about the end of the affair.'

Ivor drew a deep breath. 'I don't want to sound
unsympathetic, but what did she expect?' he said gently.
'They made no promises to each other and Katie hasn't
exactly been living the life of a nun, has she? Perhaps I
sound cynical but, as my old Dad used to say when we
were late getting to the Underground station and the
guard closed the carriage doors just as we got down to the
platform, "Son, don't worry, there's always another
train".'

There was silence for a moment and then Ivor was
startled to hear Katie's voice float across the room. He
looked up to see the tall, coltish girl standing almost in
front of him. 'You don't really believe that, Ivor, do you?
You're just saying that to make me feel better,' she said
morosely.

'I *do* mean it, Katie,' he said firmly. 'There are plenty
more fish in the sea, especially for gorgeous girls like you
and Sam. Here, did either of you do Latin at school? No?

150

I don't remember much myself except one of old Horace's Odes which goes *Carpe diem, quam minimum credula postero.*'

The girls looked blankly at him until he translated: '"Seize the present day, trusting the morrow as little as possible." Come on, Katie, there's a certain little knob I want you to twiddle!' This unexpected invitation cheered Katie up and she giggled: 'Ivor, you naughty boy, I never knew you cared!'

'Well, truth will out,' he laughed, rising from his seat. 'But I was thinking of the knob on your radio, switch it on and tune it in to Radio Luxembourg! I know that Ruff Trayde's new single *Waiting and Watching* is being heavily plugged by the record company all this week and I'd very much like to hear it.'

'What a good idea, Ivor,' Sam said, rising to her feet. 'Though for a moment you had me worried! Katie, would you like some tea?'

Katie switched on the radio. As Ivor had requested, she tuned it to the pop music station. 'I wouldn't mind a drink, Sam, let's open that bottle of champagne we've had in the fridge for yonks. Ivor's got the right idea. Let's have a party!'

Katie dashed into the kitchen and brought back one of the three bottles of Moet & Chandon which Harold Godfrey had presented to her for working through the weekend on an audit for an important client. 'Get the glasses ready,' she ordered and unwrapped the foil around the cork. With a 'pop' she opened the bottle and the three of them drank a toast to the future. They rocked to the music of The Beatles and The Rolling Stones and Ivor cuddled both girls close to him as they swayed to the wistful melody of Ruff Trayde's new record.

'It's a good song but a little sad,' said Sam. 'I think Ruff's better with something more lively. You work for his agent, don't you?'

'Yes, but I only look after his publicity. So if you're not keen on the record, don't hold it against me.'

Katie had drunk the lion's share of the champagne and she giggled a little tipsily: 'Don't worry, Ivor, you can hold anything against me any time you like.'

'Jolly good, Katie, you make a clean breast of it.'

'Maybe I will,' she replied spiritedly. 'I'm going to open another bottle.' She came back and sat down as she fiddled with the recalcitrant cork. 'I can't get the damn thing open,' she frowned and Ivor looked at her in alarm as she shook the bottle to try and dislodge the bung.

'Mind where you're aiming that cork, u-r-g-h!' gurgled Ivor as the cork shot out of the bottle and caught him squarely in the balls. He was more startled than hurt but Ivor could not resist making more of his injury than was strictly necessary. He clapped his hands over his groin as he collapsed to the floor as the girls shrieked with laughter. 'I'm so pleased you find it so funny,' he groaned. 'Perhaps Katie would like to bring another bottle out for an action replay!'

'Oh, you're not really hurt, are you?' said Sam as she and Katie knelt down over him. 'No, just maimed for life,' said Ivor airily, pulling Sam's hand down to caress the damaged area. She smoothed her palm along his cock but Katie was even keener to discover if she could help ease Ivor's discomfort. She unbuckled his belt and deftly unbuttoned the waistband of his trousers.

'We'd better see for ourselves that Ivor's tackle is still in good working order,' she explained as she switched her attention to loosening his tie and unbuttoning his shirt before unzipping his fly.

Sam brushed back the long strands of blonde hair which had fallen down over her face before she helped Katie undress the willing Ivor. He lifted his bottom from the carpet to assist them lift his legs out of his trousers.

'I'll look after his cock if you'll take care of his balls,' said Sam as they rolled down Ivor's underpants and pulled them over his ankles. His naked penis began to swell to an immense size when Sam clasped his cock in her hands and moved them slowly up and down the fast hardening shaft. Katie lowered her head and began to tongue his hairy ballsack with long, langorous strokes which made Ivor shiver with delight.

Very soon Sam's tousled mane was jostling with Katie's head of dark, silky hair as the blonde girl kissed his knob and swirled her tongue across the smooth mushroom dome of his uncapped helmet. Katie was now lustily lapping his balls and Ivor reached down and clutched their heads as he lay back, almost swooning with excitement whilst the two pairs of soft lips brought him all too quickly to an electric climax. Ivor gasped as the thrilling wave of jism flooded along his shaft and burst out into Sam's mouth. Swallowing and sucking, she gulped down his salty ejaculation and when Sam lifted her head, Katie took her place, squeezing his twitching tool and lapping up the last few drops of milky spunk from the now wilting crown of his cock.

Sam gave a small hiccup and Katie looked across mischievously and quipped: 'Naughty girl, don't you remember Nanny telling you that every mouthful must be well chewed before swallowing.'

'Another glass of champagne should do the trick,' panted Ivor, his chest heaving as he struggled to sit up, as he added: 'I wouldn't mind another swig myself.'

But Katie demurred with a chuckle. 'Please don't have any more, Ivor. Too much bubbly will affect your darling prick, which still has lots more work to get through tonight.

'You stay there and recover while Sam and I get undressed. We'll call you in when we're ready.'

He grinned and waited as he heard the girls whisper behind the closed door of Katie's bedroom. A couple of minutes later Katie called out: 'We're ready for you, lover boy' and he padded across the room and flung open the door. He stood transfixed at the erotic tableau being played out in front of him. The two girls, both stark naked, were cuddling each other lasciviously on the bed.

He sat down on the soft mattress and licked his lips as he compared the tufty blonde curls of Sam's pubic mound with Katie's abundant, silky black bush through which he could clearly see her pouting pussy lips.

'I've always wanted to suck Sam's pussy whilst being fucked,' said Katie dreamily. 'I'll start the ball rolling and then I'll rely on you, Ivor, to carry on the good work.'

She began by wetting her finger and placing it at the base of Sam's throat and then slowly, very slowly she traced a line down Sam's exquisitely white body, keeping her finger wet as it journeyed across her breasts, tweaking the erect nipples before passing over her flat belly and down into the curly grotto of her pussy hair. As she ground her palm against Sam's pubic mound, the blonde girl quivered with anticipation. Katie cupped Sam's breast with her left hand and murmured: 'Oooh, it turns me on to feel your nips swell up in my palm. There, lovely Sam, don't you just adore having your titties and cunt rubbed at the same time?'

'Oh yes,' gasped Sam as carefully Katie slid her knuckles around her reddening cunny lips. Her legs parted and she groaned: 'Ohhh . . . ohhh . . . that feels so good . . . please, darling, finish me off! I want your wicked little tongue inside me, licking my clitty!'

Katie continued to frig her tingling honeypot as she scrambled between her legs. Sam grabbed her head in her hands as Katie now buried her mouth in the succulent, moist padding of blonde curls. Ivor's prick began to stir as he watched Katie kiss Sam's sweet pussy. She thrust her questing tongue into the hot, wet hole, licking and lapping furiously whilst teasing the hard ball of her clitty with her finger. This made Sam whimper with unabashed delight.

He moved behind Katie, pulling on his shaft until it stood proudly up almost against his tummy. He parted the soft sumptuous bum cheeks and glimpsing her furry crack slid his shaft in the inviting cleft. She raised her buttocks slightly, showing her cunt to be wet and open, spread like a flower as she reached round for his prick and guided it home. With one vigorous shove Ivor buried his not inconsiderable shaft to the hilt, his balls flapping against the back of Katie's thighs. He thrust again and again, his hands first caressing her breasts and then sliding into her cunt to join his cock. He thrust again and again and he clasped the wriggling girl to him, whilst Sam's legs threshed wildly and she screamed out: 'Yes! Yes! I'm there!' as Katie brought her off to a rousing climax.

Ivor continued to work his shaft in and out of Katie's cunt from behind and she worked her bottom from side to side so that he could embed every inch of his pulsating prick as her cunt magically expanded to receive it. Her buttocks rotated as his rigid rod rammed home and Ivor slipped into the delicious feeling of an impending come. He postponed the orgasm by slowing the rhythm, waiting until Katie's moans grew higher and then pumping rapidly. Then he spunked in a great shudder, a fountain of jism pouring out of his agitated cock just as Katie gurgled with joy as she too reached the pinnacle of pleasure.

They spent the rest of the night tucked up in Katie's bed. Ivor reflected that for the second time running, he was sharing a bed with two gorgeous girls, having spent the previous night with Naomi and Babs. It's unfair to compare, he mused, though he wondered what it would be like to cavort with all four in one of the big circular beds he had seen advertised in *Playboy*. No, one could even have too much fucking, he decided, though no doubt his exhausted prick would doubtless be straining to rise to the occasion in the cold light of morning!

Fortunately he woke with the dawn. As usual his cock was as hard as nails, but he looked at his watch and decided he would have to forgo the pleasure of an early morning session of love-making. Both girls were fast asleep so Ivor gathered his clothes in his hands and dressed himself in the lounge. It was only half past six so he'd have time to change and bathe but he felt awkward about leaving them without even a word of thanks. He gnawed his lower lip and then his face brightened as he noticed David Nash's letter to Katie on the table. He fished out a pen from his pocket and scribbled on the back of one of the sheets: *Have had to dash – you both looked so lovely and peaceful I didn't have the heart to wake you up! Sam, I'll call you tomorrow night! Luv, Ivor.* He placed the paper in the middle of the table and set two glasses on either side to make sure it didn't flutter to the floor.

Very quietly, he opened the front door and closed it behind him with equal care. Noiselessly he went down the short flight of stairs. As he was about to open the front door, he heard the noise of another door opening and a female voice called out: 'Hello there, can you hold on a moment.'

He turned to his right and saw a pretty, buxom girl wearing a tight-fitting short dressing gown who had opened the door of the ground floor apartment. Her face was vaguely familiar to Ivor, who politely waited to see what she wanted from him.

'Hi, have you just come upstairs from Katie and Sam's place?' she said pleasantly. 'You must have really enjoyed your stay. Katie's bedroom is directly over mine and I heard the three of you fooling around well after one o'clock.'

Ivor blushed but the girl smiled and said ruefully: 'Oh, please don't worry, I don't want to hassle you about it. Honestly, you didn't disturb me at all, worse luck, because, would you believe, my new boy friend, aged twenty eight and a half, had to leave me at midnight and go back home to his parents!'

This information triggered off activity in Ivor's little grey cells and he snapped his fingers. 'We've met before, haven't we? Didn't I see you at the Anthony Group twenty-fifth anniversary party in Elstree a couple of weeks ago?'

'Yes, I was there, but I'll be honest, I don't remember meeting you,' she confessed, with a confused look on her face.

'We weren't actually introduced but I never forget a pretty face,' said Ivor. 'I know that's one of the oldest clichés in the book but it's true so I haven't any choice but to use it. But I know your name's Maggie and that you're Mr Martin's personal secretary.'

She cleared some stray auburn hair from her forehead. 'You *are* a clever chap. I wish I could remember names and faces so effortlessly.' Ivor chuckled and said: 'I cannot tell a lie, ma'am – I did remember your face but Sam told me your name last night.'

Maggie returned his laugh and said: 'Oh dear, now I'm really embarrassed – I suppose she called me Maggie the Moaner! No, go on, you can admit it, I promise you that Sam, Katie and I aren't at each other's throats, even though they say I drive them crazy when they hear me making love. Actually, when I heard someone walk across the hall to the front door I opened my door to see if it was the mystery guest who could pass on a message to Sam and Katie about the pot not calling the kettle black after last night's shenanigans. I dare say they're still fast asleep?'

'Well, I certainly owe you an apology for disturbing your rest, especially as you have to get up so early,' said Ivor gallantly. But the attractive girl insisted that no damage had been done. 'I'm always up at this time,' she explained. 'Look, I've just made a pot of fresh coffee – would you like to join me in a cup?'

Ivor hesitated but he liked Maggie's friendly, relaxed manner as well as her curvey figure, which was accentuated by her tight, short cream robe. 'Thanks, I'd love to,' he said and followed her into her flat. 'My name's Ivor, by the way, Ivor Belling and I work for your Group's public relations consultants.'

'Nice to meet you, Ivor. So you're with Cable Publicity then? Mr Martin thinks very highly of your firm. Do you work on our account?'

'No, young Graeme Johnstone's in charge of your account. But I keep an occasional eye over what's going on and I was delighted to come to your party. But most of my work is in our consumer division with the Bob Maxwell Entertainment Organisation.'

She looked across to him with a wry smile. 'Bob Maxwell, isn't he the man with a stable of pop singers? That sounds much more interesting than working with us! There isn't much glamour in manufacturing venetian blinds!'

'There may be some glamour but there's lots more aggravation, with all those snotty-nosed kids who think they're God's gift to the music business after their first record's been released.'

'Oh, I hope Ruff Trayde's not like that, he's always been one of my favourite singers,' said Maggie, pushing a mug of steaming hot coffee across the table. 'Here, would you like some toast too, I was going to pop a couple of slices under the grill.'

'Thanks, I'm feeling quite hungry,' said Ivor gratefully. 'Anyhow, Ruff's an exception to the rule, he's a nice, level-headed young man.'

'Well, I'm pleased to hear it. I only wish I could say the same about my boy friend! Mind you, I shouldn't say too much about Brian as you probably know him quite well. He does a lot of work for Cable Publicity.'

'Brian? Brian Lipman?' cried Ivor, struggling not to laugh. 'Well, of course I know him – why we had lunch together only yesterday. What a coincidence! Look, it's nothing to do with me, but you must know that Brian's only staying with his parents whilst the builders are working in his apartment. There's been a problem with subsidence and the whole block of flats needed underpinning. His place is on the ground floor so Brian decided to move out for a month and let the builders get on with it.'

Maggie growled as she switched on the grill and slid the tray under the electric bars. 'I heard all about that business,' she admitted, 'I offered him the chance to stay here. But even if he'd accepted, he'd go home to eat at least every Friday night. And did you know that Brian speaks to his Mum every day – he even called her when we went down to Wiltshire for the weekend!'

Ivor couldn't prevent his amusement showing as he tried to console her. 'Maggie, obviously you're not used to going out with a nice Jewish boy! Sorry, love, but I have to tell you that what you've described is about par for the course.'

She let out a deep sigh and said: 'Yes, I know, my Mum's Italian and her lot are just as bad. Do you know, she still talks with tears in her eyes about the day I moved out to live on my own.

'Still, to be fair about it, although I was cross with Brian about leaving me after we'd made love – it made me feel as if I were at the end of a wham, bam, thank you ma'am affair – the real reason why I was so jealous of what was happening upstairs with you and the girls was that Brian and I had a silly row about sex, so we didn't even have a farewell fuck before he left.'

She pursed her lips in a wilful pout and added: 'Looking back, we both behaved childishly. After all, it was really so silly to argue about such a trivial business.'

'Go on, Maggie,' prompted Ivor, 'it may have been trivial but I'm sure you'd still appreciate an unbiased opinion from an independent judge. I've no axe to grind – Brian's an old mate but you've provided me with breakfast!'

Maggie looked at him admiringly. 'I was right when I said you were a clever boy,' she remarked as she flipped over the bread on the grill tray. 'I'll tell you what it was all about – though really it was such a trivial business. Brian told me that he read somewhere that you could tell the size of a man's prick by the size of his nose. I said that in my limited experience that didn't hold true. What I *have* found, though, was that you can usually tell the size of a fella's shaft by looking at his fingers. Long straight fingers equal a long straight cock, short stubby fingers equal a short stubby staff, and so on.

'Of course Brian didn't like to hear that theory, because

his fingers are a bit on the short side. One thing led to another and we had a blazing row.'

Ivor spread out his hands in sympathy. 'What can I say?' he murmured, pressing his hand on top of hers. 'Fellows are the same. There's an old Army saying which goes "like titties, like clitty" so if a girl has big nipples . . .' His voice trailed off and then he added: 'The trouble is that people are always trying to find out what's in the package without having to unwrap it first.'

'You're not wrong, Ivor – though half the fun of receiving a parcel is to find out what's inside.' She looked lasciviously down at Ivor's lap. 'Now your nose is only of average size, but you have nice, long fingers. If what Brian read is right, you'll only have a medium-sized prick. But if *my* theory is correct, then you should have a lovely thick cock and big hairy balls.'

He looked squarely at the luscious girl who parted the lapels of her dressing gown so that Ivor could see the swell of her full breasts. 'Don't you think you should find out for yourself? After all, it would settle the argument if nothing else,' suggested Ivor. His prick tingled as it started to swell and bound inside his trousers.

'Sounds like a good idea to me,' said Maggie, licking her upper lip with her tongue. 'Let me just turn off the grill. Come in to the bedroom, Ivor, and do please excuse the mess.'

He followed her into the bedroom and without further preliminaries she unknotted the cord of her robe, letting the garment slide down and reveal that underneath it she was totally nude. Maggie sensed Ivor's excitement at seeing her beautiful bare bottom and she deliberately accentuated the well-shaped white cheeks of her delicious bum by wiggling her hips in front of him. Then she turned and displayed her large cherry topped breasts and well covered pussy. Ivor noticed that her pubic hair was fashioned into a heart-shaped curve.

'Well now, let's see who's right,' Maggie murmured throatily as she sank to her knees and unbuckled Ivor's belt. He jerked down the zip of his trousers himself and she tugged them down with his underpants. As his cock sprang up, it narrowly missed hitting her eye. 'Oh my, I win, there can't be any doubt about it,' she cooed as she took his pulsating stiff cock in her hand and rubbed the shaft fiercely up and down, capping and uncapping his purple helmet. 'Don't go away, I've a tape measure on my dressing-table.'

Moments later she was measuring his rigid prick and with a little cry she declared: 'Eight and three quarter inches! What a whopper! But you're not so big as my friend Richard. Old Donkey Dick, as I call him, has a cock almost ten inches long and even thicker than yours. But it's how you use your equipment which really matters.'

'Absolutely so, and a good workman never blames his tool!' said Ivor decisively, placing his hands on the gorgeous girl's shoulders and making her walk backwards for a few steps until she fell back on the bed.

Without ado she ran her hand down to her pussy and stroked a finger down her moistening slit. Ivor could see the red chink inside the curly grotto of her pubic mound as she invited him with her sensuous eyes to join her. He complied with her unspoken request and their mouths closed, their lips sucking quietly and urgently, their tongues licking wetly together, tasting the hot desire which was starting to course through their bodies, needing only the briefest coaxing to speed through to a frenetic fulfilment.

Abruptly, she broke off the kiss to murmur: 'I'm going to milk this monster dry' as she jerked her hand up and down his hot, smooth-skinned penis.

Ivor gritted his teeth as he tried to contain the anticipatory tingle which was now surging through his shaft. 'Maggie, we shouldn't be doing this. I might well see Brian Lipman today. How will I be able to look him in the eye?'

'Don't be silly,' she said with a scornful chuckle. 'Do

you think I don't know he fucks almost every girl that comes into his studio? He's even screwed half the girls at Cable Publicity. We have a very open relationship and it's okay with me so long as he doesn't get emotionally involved.'

She leaned forward and opened her mouth to take his hard, throbbing tool between her lips. She sucked lustily on his rounded knob, savouring the flavour of his cock, rolling her tongue over the domed helmet as she eased another three inches down her throat. Her hands circled the pulsating pole, working the velvet skin up and down whilst she began to bob her head up and down in a sensuous rhythm. She cupped his hairy balls in her other hand and purred contentedly as Ivor slid his hand down to finger her damp pussy.

'Your cunt's sopping wet, you naughty girl,' he murmured in her ear, nipping the pink lobe with his teeth. 'How would you like my big, fat prick in your honeypot? Isn't that what you really want?'

She looked up at him with shining moist eyes and released his glistening shaft from her mouth. 'Yes, oh yes!' she panted. 'Please scew me! Stick that lovely cock in my cunt, you randy fucker!'

'Of course,' whispered Ivor wickedly. 'But first, a word from our sponsor.'

He pulled her across him and, lifting her dripping crack directly over his mouth, buried his face in her bushy mound. She screamed with delight as he lustily lapped the love juice which was pouring from her cunt. She writhed in ecstacy as he sucked furiously on her burgeoning clitty, which fairly throbbed as he playfully nibbled on the erectile rubbery flesh.

'Fuck me, fuck me!' she yelled. She threw herself down on the bed and opened her legs to await the arrival of Ivor's huge prick. He twisted over and, taking hold of his shaft, nudged his knob against her yearning cunny lips. He pulled back, wickedly relishing the pleading eagerness of the excited girl as she waited for his inward thrust. He sank forward and she was so juicy that her cunt enveloped his cock like a wet, warm glove, sliding deep, deep between the clinging walls of her love tunnel.

'Eeeeee! Eeeeee!' she cried out loudly, writhing in uncontrolled delight as Ivor's shaft sank thrillingly home. His buttocks rose and fell, his muscular, lean limbs shuddering as he drove his cock harder and harder into her cunny, bringing her swiftly to fresh peaks of pleasure. She shouted with joy as a series of orgasmic ripples crackled through her body. She pumped her creaming cunt against his cock and so tightly were their bodies joined that Ivor felt that his penis was somehow welded to her agitated slit.

He paused to catch his breath and then ploughed on, filling Maggie's crack with the thick prick which she craved so urgently until finally she screamed out with sheer excitement and with one final, almighty heave he followed her to a glorious orgasm. The hot, sticky cream burst out of his cock, drenching the long funnel of her cunt as Ivor spent himself to the limit, riding stiffly in and out of her slit until he was milked dry. He withdrew his deflated shaft and lay back with glazed eyes, his heart pounding and chest heaving as he panted with exhaustion.

They lay in silence and it crossed Ivor's mind that Sam and Katie had probably heard Maggie's screeches whilst they were fucking. If they cross-examined him, it would take some explaining away, he thought.

Maggie broke his reverie when she giggled and said: 'Now you must have a proper breakfast before you go. There's nothing like a good fuck for whetting the appetite.'

She was as expert in the kitchen as she was in bed and soon Ivor was tucking into a fluffy cheese omelette with lashings of hot, buttered toast, washed down by two mugs of fresh, aromatic coffee.

'You're welcome to come back any time you're passing,' she said hospitably as he struggled into his raincoat. 'And don't worry – I won't tell Sam or Katie if you don't tell Brian. As I told you, we have an open relationship but I prefer to keep my love life as private as possible.'

'Of course,' Ivor promised as he kissed her cheek and hurried quickly out of the house, worried that Sam or Katie might see him drive away. But as he waited for the traffic to clear at the junction at the end of the street, his eye wandered across to a girl standing on the corner of the road. He peered closely at her and thought hard. Then he clicked his fingers in triumph . . .

Unless he was greatly mistaken, those large blue eyes in an oval face, framed by cascades of long blonde hair, that full, pouting mouth belonged to the spirited girl who, the other morning, had been the only person in the train carriage to help him in his battle with the young hooligan.

The girl must be waiting for a lift, he reasoned, for she was not wearing a topcoat but was dressed in tight, white trousers and a light green jacket and was pacing impatiently up and down the pavement.

Ivor swung his car into the kerb and pulled up beside her. He got out and walked towards the girl who was now consulting her watch. 'Excuse me, but aren't you the brave lady who came to my aid on the Bakerloo line yesterday morning?'

She looked blankly at him for a moment and then her face cleared and as she smiled, two delicious dimples formed at the sides of her generous mouth. 'Goodness me, it's Sir Galahad of West Hampstead, we meet again, sirrah,' she said. Ivor acknowledged the compliment with a low bow, doffing an imaginary hat.

'Has your coach not arrived, fair maiden?' he enquired as he straightened up. 'I can take you to the Underground Station or, if you can wait ten minutes whilst I shower and change, I'm taking my car into town. My office is in Holborn if that's any use to you.'

'You're very kind, Sir Galahad,' she replied. 'Funnily enough, I have an audition in Holborn this morning and a friend was going to take me in by car but he hasn't turned up.'

'An audition? Are you in show business? Now I come to think of it, your face is very familiar.'

'Is it? But I'm not an actress, I'm a model.'

Ivor looked at her again and wondered whether the gods were still smiling upon him. 'You wouldn't be with Leon Standlake's Churchmill Agency by any chance?' he said, his heart starting to beat faster.

'Yes I am, but how on earth did you know that?' she said in astonishment. 'I know even more about you,' Ivor continued triumphantly. 'You have an appointment to see the executive at Cable Publicity who's looking for a girl to promote a brand of tan-without-sun pills.'

She threw back her head and laughed out loud. 'This is crazy! Are you some kind of mind-reader?'

Ivor opened the door of his car and invited her to take a seat. 'No, but give me five minutes and I'll explain all,' he said, girding his loins for what promised to be a busy but rewarding morning . . .